Christmas at the Rekindle Inn

by

Lori Waters

Christmas at the Rekindle Inn

Cover Art by *Kristian Norris*

The Wild Rose Press, Inc.
PO Box 708
Adams Basin, NY 14410-0708
Visit us at www.thewildrosepress.com

Publishing History
First Champagne Rose Edition, 2015
Print ISBN 978-1-5092-0509-7
Digital ISBN 978-1-5092-0510-3

Published in the United States of America

...his eyes scanned the room.

Had his body tensed the second he recognized her?

Her heart plummeted. Why did she care if he was happy to see her?

He closed the distance in a few long strides, stealing the breath from her lungs with every step. "Hey." JT slid onto the barstool beside her.

"Hey."

He flagged down the bartender. "Can I get a draft?" His gaze loomed over her empty glass. "Make that two."

The bartender waited for her approval. She nodded, and the big guy snatched her mug and turned to the tap.

"I started to think you weren't coming."

JT frowned. "Yeah, sorry. Got held up at work."

"There's a surprise."

"Wow. I've missed that sarcasm."

Her stomach tightened. Why had she said that? She could care less how much time he put in at the job these days as long as she didn't have to stay up nights waiting for him anymore. Afraid he'd been hurt on the job or worse. Nope. Her days of worrying over Joseph Tanner Walker and his workaholic ways were behind her. He could live in the site trailer for all she cared.

"So what's up? I'm guessing you received the so-called *present* from the folks?" He slipped off his jacket and slung it onto an empty stool before propping huge flannelled biceps on the bar. Mary caught the familiar whiff of musk and soap.

She picked up her brochure of said Christmas present, and fanned herself. The bar was stifling. What'd they have the thermostat set on—order another cold beer?

Kudos for Lori Waters

2014 TARA Award Winner in the Series Contemporary category for *CHRISTMAS AT THE REKINDLE INN.*

~*~

"Lori Waters wraps romance in a beautiful bow in this heart-warming love story set in a charming winter Wonderland."

~author Elizabeth Michels

~*~

"*CHRISTMAS AT THE REKINDLE INN* is a heart-warming debut filled with charm, engaging characters, and Christmas magic. Ms. Waters wrote an engaging tale of a place I loved visiting, and I think you'll enjoy the trip, too."

~author Ashantay Peters

Dedication

For my Mom. I love you to Heaven and back.

Acknowledgments

I would like to thank my husband and children, Timmy, Rachel, and Jacob, for always believing in me.

Thanks to my dad, who told me after reading a short story I wrote in high school, "You should be a writer when you grow up."

I'd like to thank my family and friends for sharing my dream with me for all these years.

Thanks to my fantastic and patient critique partners, Ashantay Peters, Elizabeth Michels, Ann Chaney, and Robin.

Thanks to my blog partners and dear friends, the beautiful and extremely awesome Bad Girlz!

Thanks to my talented editor, Melanie Billings, and everyone involved at The Wild Rose Press.

And most importantly, thanks to my Lord for making all this possible.

Chapter 1

He was going to stand her up.

Great. Mary Walker tapped her fingers on the side of her glass. The neon clock behind the O'Malley's bar showed seven thirty-four.

"Can I get you another one?" The bartender, a big guy, pointed to her nearly empty beer mug. Not bad looking if a girl could get past the skull tattoos plastered down his arms. The red Santa hat sitting on the side of his bald head was almost amusing.

"Better not. I'm meeting my husband." She needed to stop saying that. "I mean my ex-husband. Technically, he's not officially my ex yet. He will be in a month." She drained the last few sips from her mug. "I guess you could consider him my ex if you wanted. Yeah, let's say he's my ex."

The bartender leaned his giant frame onto the bar and raised a brow.

Uh-oh.

"Maybe I can get you something else then?" His lips curved into a frisky grin. "Anything?"

She glanced at the black ink lettering on the top of his left hand that read *TROUBLE*. Like he needed to spell it out.

"Well?" A silver tongue ring slid over his bottom lip.

Yikes.

She shook her head so fast, her dangling earrings smacked the sides of her cheeks. He chuckled and then moved to wait on a platinum blonde sitting at the other end of the bar.

Mary tried to ignore her reflection bouncing off the huge mirror behind the bar. If she looked too closely she might see the faint wrinkles fanned around her eyes—stress damage caused by her separation. Or was it the excitement of seeing JT again that had her avoiding her image?

She focused on the silver garland hung unevenly around the edges of the glass. The words "Merry Christmas" painted with spray-can snow in the center. December already. How had her favorite time of year slipped in without notice?

One more regrettable thing that came with divorce. The routines she and JT had spent years perfecting became obsolete overnight. No Christmas Eve party at the in-laws. No Christmas morning mimosas while exchanging presents. No hosting Christmas dinner for their parents. Her finger ran over the sapphire and diamond bracelet wrapped around her wrist. Last year's present from JT. She needed to start over. New Christmas traditions without him.

She blinked away tears. Divorce sucked.

Her pulse shot up a notch when she spotted JT's large frame in the mirror. Six months since she'd seen him last. Mary sighed. *Here we go.*

He ran a hand through his dark, wind-tossed hair, and his eyes scanned the room. Had his body tensed the second he recognized her?

Her heart plummeted. Why did she care if he was happy to see her?

He closed the distance in a few long strides, stealing the breath from her lungs with every step. "Hey." JT slid onto the barstool beside her.

"Hey."

He flagged down the bartender. "Can I get a draft?" His gaze loomed over her empty glass. "Make that two."

The bartender waited for her approval. She nodded, and the big guy snatched her mug and turned to the tap.

"I started to think you weren't coming."

JT frowned. "Yeah, sorry. Got held up at work."

"There's a surprise."

"Wow. I've missed that sarcasm."

Her stomach tightened. Why had she said that? She could care less how much time he put in at the job these days as long as she didn't have to stay up nights waiting for him anymore. Afraid he'd been hurt on the job or worse. Nope. Her days of worrying over Joseph Tanner Walker and his workaholic ways were behind her. He could live in the site trailer for all she cared.

"So what's up? I'm guessing you received the so-called *present* from the folks?" He slipped off his jacket and slung it onto an empty stool before propping huge flannelled biceps on the bar. Mary caught the familiar whiff of musk and soap.

She picked up her brochure of said Christmas present, and fanned herself. The bar was stifling. What'd they have the thermostat set on—order another cold beer?

"It's obvious our mothers have lost their minds if they think we would even consider going." She waved the pamphlet toward him.

"No thanks. I've got my own." The bartender

barely had time to set down the mugs before JT grabbed his beer, took a big gulp, and drained a third before setting it back down. His hand swiped away the foam mustache. "There's no way we can accept this gift."

There's one thing they could agree on.

"Have you told your mom you're not going?" she asked.

"No."

"Why not?" She winced. Her words sounded whinier than she'd intended.

"I haven't had a chance to call her. I've been trying to wrap up this job before we shut down for the holidays."

She glanced at him. His jaw was clenched, and he looked a little worn around the eyes. Probably the awkwardness of seeing his ex for the first time in forever. She didn't feel the least bit sorry for him. Meeting in person had been his idea.

"Well, call your mom and let her know. Then I can tell my mom." She braved eye contact. If only the little butterflies in her belly would scurry away.

JT frowned. "Just like you. Make me look bad in your mommy's eyes so you don't have to. Grow up and be your own woman, Mary." He slammed his mug on the counter causing the liquid to spill.

How could he even say that? He knew standing up to her mom had nothing to do with being *her own woman* and everything to do with not wanting to hurt her mother. Her dad had done enough damage.

She spun around on her stool, colliding with his leg. "I *am* my own woman." The overwhelming heat radiating off his thigh sent her spinning back to her original position.

He bumped a broad shoulder into hers. She'd forgotten what it was like to be near him, to feel the warmth of him at her side.

"Yeah, you think so?" he said beneath dark lashes. "Then tell me Ms. Independent, why are you waiting for me to be the bad guy? Again."

"I'm not trying to make you the bad guy. I just don't want to hurt my mom."

Awkward silence stood firm between them for the beat of a few seconds.

They picked up their beers simultaneously and took deep swigs. Mary returned her mug to the counter. "The gift's ridiculous. Do they really expect us to stay a week at some inn for Christmas? Together? A month before our divorce is final? Don't they know what they're asking?"

The answer was obvious. Their mothers had strategized a desperate plan to stop the divorce. She still couldn't believe it. They had made reservations at a quiet little place in Vermont that specialized in troubled marriages. *The Rekindle Inn*. Their marriage wasn't troubled—it was over.

"I guess it's their last ditch attempt to save us." He flashed the impish grin that always signified trouble.

"Too late."

His smile vanished. He looked like a puppy that had just been pushed out the back door at supper time.

"Personally, I think the whole thing's silly." She couldn't believe her mom's gall. Had her mother forgotten how long it had taken her to recover from leaving JT?

She hadn't slept, had barely eaten. She'd forced herself to go to work to keep from losing her job. If it hadn't been for David's persistence about going out to dinner a few months back, she'd probably still be curled up on the sofa in her pajamas watching reality show reruns. "Yeah, they've lost their minds."

"Agreed." He took another drink. He turned his gaze on her and the corner of his mouth curved. "I bet your little lawyer boyfriend isn't too crazy about the idea."

Apparently small town gossip left nothing untold. Mary didn't really want to get into a conversation about her boyfriend with her husband. Ex-husband. She wouldn't back down either. "What does David have to do with anything?"

"I'm guessing, *a lot*?"

"You're wrong. If I wanted to go, David wouldn't say a thing."

JT laughed. "He'd have plenty to say, all right. You, being cooped up in some cozy inn with your ex for a week." He chuckled again.

"He'd be fine with it." She crossed her arms and perched on her stool. "How about Whitney Conner? I'm sure she wouldn't be too pleased."

"Whitney?"

"I heard she moved back from New York." Why that fact drove her absolutely bonkers remained unclear.

"So?"

Did he really think she wouldn't figure it out? JT and Whitney dated all through high school, until they broke up to attend different colleges. Whitney was back. Mary was out of the picture—duh. "You're going to tell me you haven't seen her?"

"Of course I've seen her. She's my boss's daughter."

She'd been plenty jealous of Whitney Conner during the past five years. Mary swallowed down the green giant trying to escape from the pit of old habit. Every time the girl came for a visit, Mary had freaked out. Worried JT would cheat on her like her dad cheated on her mother. But all of that had stopped being her problem.

JT picked up the brochure of the Rekindle Inn and scanned the front. "I wonder how much money they spent on this place."

A pinch of guilt squeezed her insides. Her mom definitely didn't have money to throw away. "You think they can get a refund?"

"Doubt it. Not this late in the game."

The picture of the snow-covered town plastered on the cover looked beautiful. Exactly how she'd imagined the North Pole as a child. "They should have talked to us first." She inhaled deeply and the musty smell of sour bar floor stung her nose. "Maybe it's not too late. If you call your mom now, they can try to get their money back."

His eyes lit up. "Nope. You call your mom first."

"No."

"Then I won't either. I'm not getting you out of this one. I took the heat for five years with your mom. Every time she wanted you to do something you didn't want to do, you used me as an excuse." He shot her a stubborn smirk. "Nope. I'm not doing it. You don't want to go, you tell your mom the truth."

Maybe Mary deserved his obnoxious resistance. She *had* let JT be the fall guy when she didn't want to go along with her mother's schemes, but she hadn't done it on purpose. She just didn't want to cause her mom more unhappiness.

She locked eyes with him. "Let me get this straight. You're implying that if I refuse to tell my mom I don't want to go, you'll go to the Rekindle Inn?"

His head tilted to the side. "I…maybe…" After a second, his smile widened revealing his perfectly straight teeth. "Yep."

No way. He bluffed. He'd never go.

She nibbled at the corner of her lip contemplating her next move. Two could play that game. "Then pack your bags, buddy boy." She patted him on the shoulder. "Looks like we're spending our Christmas vacations in Jollyville, Vermont." That would surely instigate his retreat.

Amusement drained from his face. "Are you serious? You'd suffer a week in Vermont with me, just because you're too chicken to stand up to your mom?"

Her stomach knotted. It did sound ridiculous when he said the words aloud. Would she really go on the stupid trip to keep from disappointing her mother? Absurd, but, yes, she would.

Wait. She only needed to pretend until he backed down. He'd surely back down.

"No, JT. Not because I'm chicken. I'll suffer a week with you because I don't want our parents to waste their money." She tilted her head to the side. "I'll suffer a week with you because after one long, dreadful week, I'll finally be rid of you."

His expression said it all. She'd shocked him. That should do it. He'd be running for the hills any second. At least for his cell to call his mother and decline the Christmas present.

He recovered quickly. "Guess I'll see you next

week. Want me to swing by and pick you up on my way to the airport?"

Darn his stubborn butt. Her pulse pounded in her temples. He had to be bluffing. He'd never suffer through marriage counseling.

"No. I'll drive myself, thank you very much." She plastered a fake smile on her lips.

"Fine."

She jumped to her feet. "Fine," she repeated as she put on her coat. She slipped trembling fingers into her leather gloves. "I'll be there with jingle bells on."

A pulsing artery threatened to beat through her neck. What was she doing? Just pick up the stupid phone and explain the situation. Her mother would understand.

But the adrenaline high wouldn't let her back down from his dare. Flirty Santa noticed her stand up and hurried over. "You ready to square up your tab?"

She nodded in JT's direction. "He'll get it." She flashed a wide smile at biker bartender. "And thanks for the offer of *anything*." She winked at him for her husband's—darn it all, her ex-husband's—sake and marched out of the bar.

****

Mary held the phone six inches from her ear but could still hear David yelling, as she walked down Main Street toward her car.

"What possessed you to agree to such an outrageous trip? You call JT and tell him you've reconsidered."

Cower to JT's challenge? Never. "David. It'll be fine. I'll go sit in my room for a week. I'll take work with me. I probably won't even see him." Plus, her mom would be happy and that's all that really mattered.

"No. I won't have it."

She froze, her body turning to ice. "Excuse me. What do you mean *you won't have it*?"

"I mean it's Christmas." His rigid tone softened. "I want to be with my girlfriend for the holidays. Is that so much to ask?"

"It's actually the week before. I'll be back by Christmas Eve." She knew that wouldn't appease him. The truth was she'd rather upset David than her mother. She reached her car and slipped in, thankful for the warmth.

"Look, I know this is a lot to take. It's a lot for me, too. But I need to do this for my mother." His silence was deafening. She glanced at her watch and turned the ignition. "We can talk about this later. I'm meeting Mom for dinner. I'm already late."

"By all means, you better go. We wouldn't want to upset the warden."

She gasped. "That's not very nice." Her mother could be demanding, and maybe Mary gave into her too much, but David's remark was just mean.

He sighed. "I guess I'm not feeling very nice. Go to dinner and tell her you're not going. Please, Mary. Stand up to her."

She clasped tight fingers around the steering wheel. She was tired of everyone telling her how to handle her mother. "So, instead of letting Mom tell me what to do, I'm supposed to let *you* tell me what to do?" She shifted the car into drive. "I've got to go." She pushed the end call button before he had a chance to reply.

The drive to the restaurant left too much time alone with her thoughts. Traipsing up north with JT would put a big kink in David's plans. He planned to propose for Christmas, she knew it. He'd been dropping hints for the last month. She wasn't even done with her first mess. Plus, they'd only been dating three months. What could he be thinking? She sighed. David was a great guy. Some would say the perfect package. If only she could stick that particular present back under the tree for a while.

****

JT leaned against his bar stool and watched his best friend Kyle run every striped ball on the pool table.

"So you really agreed to go?" Kyle asked and then took a shot at the eight ball.

"Yep."

"You're going to Vermont with Mary?"

"Yep."

Kyle straightened after missing the shot. "This is crazy. I thought you were done trying to crack that safe."

JT grinned. "What can I say?" He pushed off his stool to take his turn.

He missed.

"What'd she do to you, man?" Kyle grinned and took another stab at the eight ball, dropping it in the corner pocket. "You've never let me whip up on you like you have tonight."

JT rolled that question over in his brain. What'd she do to him? Who knew? Made him rethink the entire divorce.

His gut tensed. He had to fight the urge to grab her in his arms and plop a wet kiss on her at the bar earlier—more than once. That snug red sweater she'd worn hadn't helped. He readjusted his stance as his groin responded to the memory. Whenever she shot that pissed off, smoldering blue gaze his way, he was a goner.

He ran a hand through his hair. Was he crazy? Or did she make him crazy? Damn. He'd been stupid to suggest meeting. He knew she wanted to talk about the gift. It would've been an easy fix. Tell his parents "no thanks." Reimburse them. He had the money. But nope. He had to see her one last time.

"How'd she look?" Kyle asked, dragging him back into the present. "Is she doing all right?"

JT saw the look on Kyle's face. His friend missed Mary, too. The man loved her like a little sister. Kyle thought the divorce was a huge mistake, but when she'd insisted on the separation six months ago, he stuck his loyalty flag on JT's side of the field.

JT shrugged. "What can I say? She looked great. Still driving me fricking crazy."

Kyle chuckled. "Same ol' Mary."

"There was something different about her, though. I can't quite figure out." JT pulled back a swig of his beer. "Still gorgeous. Still hard-headed."

But there was something missing in her eyes. She'd looked…sad.

Maybe he imagined the expression. Why would she be sad? She had Dorky-David. Big lawyer-man. Every woman's dream.

"So be honest, JT. How'd you feel when you saw her? You still think divorce is the way to go?"

JT jabbed him in the arm. "Dude. The divorce will be final in less than thirty days. Does it matter?"

"You didn't answer the question. I was shooting for a yes or no." Kyle shrugged. "Maybe it's a good thing y'all are taking this trip."

He didn't really want to explain the millions of reasons going to Vermont with Mary wasn't a good thing, but he would. JT opened his mouth, but before he could speak, someone grabbed him from behind.

He turned. Crap. Whitney Conner.

"JT Walker, buy a girl a beer." Whitney finally released him from her death-grip.

He flagged the waitress and ordered a round.

"Hey, Kyle." The curvy brunette snatched JT's pool stick from his hand.

"What's up, Whitney?" Kyle asked, reaching for the cue ball.

She leaned over the recently racked table, revealing a lot of her own perky rack. "Let's play."

"Let's." Kyle grinned.

Whitney wasn't paying Kyle any mind. She had her eagle eyes locked on JT. The word *run* bounced into his head.

She leaned a hip against the table. "Actually, I was hoping JT could give me a lesson." She licked a teasing tongue over her shiny red lips. "It's been a while."

Kyle shot him a *there it is, all you have to do is take it* smirk.

He hadn't run into Whitney outside of work since she'd moved back from New York. She looked good on the outside, but he knew what was on the inside—one half-crazy bitch.

"Come on JT, teach me something?"

"Who are you kidding? You always knew your way around a pool table." He did his best not to give her any encouragement.

"And on top." She winked. "Come on. Let's play."

She grabbed the cue ball out of Kyle's hand and leaned over for the break, knowing perfectly well her double D's were about to spill out of her top.

Kyle mouthed the word *yikes* behind her back.

"How about we play for a shot of tequila?"

Why not? JT nodded. Whitney ran the table in a matter of minutes. Once she dropped the eight ball, she arched her brows. "You owe me a shot."

He flagged the waitress again and ordered one shot of *to-kill-ya*.

Whitney grinned. "Did you forget?" She didn't wait for an answer. "I'm good." She strutted toward him, and then whispered in his ear, "How about I refresh your memory on something else I'm pretty good at?"

On second thought, maybe tequila and Whitney Conner wasn't a good idea. Yep. Time to go. His head was full of enough crap from his meet-up with Mary. He didn't need to add Whitney Conner to the mix.

"Thanks for the offer, but I've got to go." JT almost fell, he'd backed away so fast. If the guys at work saw his retreat, they'd revoke his man card.

He walked over and slapped Kyle on the shoulder. "Why don't you give Kyle a chance? He's shooting pretty good tonight."

The way her hand tensed around that shot glass, he half expected it to come flying across the room at him.

Kyle chuckled. "Where you going, man? It's early."

"Home. I'm beat."

Kyle leaned in so only he could hear. "You scared?"

"Yep." JT grinned.

"Don't leave," Whitney protested.

"I've got an early meeting with your father in the morning."

"Tell Daddy you were with me. I can call him and reschedule for you right now." Whitney pulled her cell out of the back pocket of her painted-on jeans.

"Thanks, but I'm out." He fist bumped Kyle. "See you at work tomorrow."

"Bright and early," Kyle replied.

"See you, Whit." He dropped some money on the table for his tab, slipped his coat on and hurried out before she had a chance to follow. Maybe Mary was eager to jump into a relationship with her new big lawyer boyfriend. But he wasn't.

Chapter 2

David's BMW pulled up while Mary loaded her luggage. *Great.* He'd given her a hard time for over a week. *This should be interesting.*

He jumped out of his car and slammed the door. "So you're really going?"

Mary didn't look up. She nestled her computer bag in beside her suitcase. "Yes. I'm going." She closed the trunk and turned to face him. "I'm sorry. But I've told you a million times, you have nothing to worry about. I doubt I'll even stay the entire week." Only long enough for her mother to think she'd made an effort. She sighed, and a puff of cold air circled her face. "Who knows? Maybe I'll even get some sort of closure."

"Closure?" His eyes narrowed. "Are you insinuating you haven't closed that chapter of your life already?" After a thread of silence, he slung an arm in the air. "I don't believe this."

She leaned against the car and folded her arms. His comments weren't making the situation any easier. The trip already freaked her out. "I know what I'm doing isn't fair to you, and I don't expect you to understand, but I've got to do this." She placed a gloved hand on his chest. "If you can't accept this, I understand."

His mouth fell open. "Are you breaking up with me?"

"No. Of course not." She withdrew her hand and

slipped it in her pocket. Even though her gut screamed, *Yes! Do it now, before he proposes.*

His expression turned icy and something mean flashed in his eyes. Like a child who didn't want to share his toys. "Go. Go find your closure. Just don't take too long or I may open a chapter in someone else's book."

Had he really just said that? She fought to keep her expression blank as David jumped in his car and sped off, leaving her standing in a cloud of warm exhaust.

****

JT maneuvered his cell between his chin and shoulder as he grabbed his suitcase from the passenger seat. "Mom. Stop. Just stop." He closed the door and hit the lock button on his key-fob. "This isn't a reunion. It's a challenge of wills. Mary's only going to please her mom, and I'm only going to piss off Mary, so don't get your hopes up."

His warning didn't help. He made his way across the parking garage and to the airport entrance before his mother took a breath.

"Mom, I gotta go check in for my flight. I'll call you when I get back." He sighed. "No worries. I'll be back in time for the Christmas Eve party. Merry Christmas to you, too. I love you."

"Wait," she screamed into the receiver. "Your father just walked in and wants to talk to you."

No. Truly the last thing he needed.

"Son, you go on this trip and do what you need to do to get your wife back." His father's voice roared.

Unbelievable. "Dad, like I told Mom, the trip is a waste of time. There won't be any *getting my wife back.*"

"So you're just going to give up? You're not even going to try? Your marriage is the most important commitment you'll ever make."

The familiar disappointment punched JT in the gut. His fist clinched at his side. "Really, Dad? Because you've pounded in my head for the last ten years that working and building a career was the most important thing I'd ever do." JT stopped talking to let some man rush by him. "In fact, listening to your advice is what's got me in this situation in the first place." He didn't wait for his dad to respond. "I've got to go."

JT hung up the phone. It didn't matter what he did, nothing would be good enough for his old man. In fact, the trip would be one more thing his father could add to his *my son's not-good-enough* list. What the hell was he thinking? *Forget it.* His marriage ended six months ago when Mary kicked him out.

****

Mary scanned the seats as she passed down the aisle but didn't see JT on the plane. She arrived at her row and scooted in, thankful for the window seat. She held her breath at the cramped quarters and tried to relax. No such luck. A big knot settled between her shoulder blades. Her pulse pounded. She'd rather eat month-old sardines than fly. *You can do this.* She repeated the phrase in her mind—over and over.

Where was JT?

The longer the seat next to her remained empty, the stronger the pressure grew in her chest. She'd only flown without him once. Downing multiple shots in the airport lounge had enabled her to endure that flight. Now, she sat sober as a nun and scared out of her wits. JT always held her hand during take-off. He'd make jokes or whisper something nasty in her ear. Good Lord, what would she do?

Get off the stupid plane. That's what she could do. She unbuckled her belt and stood, but the aircraft started to move. She collapsed back in her seat.

Too late.

Her mind raced. *Don't panic. Don't panic.* The hair on the back of her neck prickled her skin. A fine bead of sweat settled over her top lip. A full-fledge panic attack loomed seconds away.

Breathe.

She closed her eyes and inhaled air in and out through her nose. The captain came over the speaker announcing take-off. Dread lodged in her throat. The motor roared, and the plane picked up speed. So did the acid churning in her belly.

Mary pressed against the back of her seat and closed her eyes tight. Clinging white knuckled fingers around the arm rest, she tried to convince herself she wasn't seconds from crashing to her fiery death. The aircraft lifted from the ground, leaving her pounding heart on the runway.

The plane began to level out, so did her nerves. She opened her eyes and glared at the empty seat beside her. She couldn't believe she'd been stuck going on this stupid trip alone. *Thanks, JT. You've made me fly alone again.*

Men. A bunch of liars.

She'd known that since her tenth birthday party. Practically the whole neighborhood had been there. The day started out to be her best birthday ever, then she'd run into the garage during a game of hide-and-seek. Her father held a woman in his arms—not her mother. His mouth had been plastered over the bimbo's, and his hands on the woman's bottom. An involuntary gasp had escaped Mary's lips, causing the two of them to break free from one another. The woman glared at Mary, straightened her clothes and stomped out the door.

Her father grabbed her shoulders. "Mary, you didn't see anything. Do you hear me?" His red and sweaty face drew closer. "You've got to promise me you won't tell your mom. You wouldn't want to cause your mom to be upset, would you?"

She had swallowed the ball of yarn caught in her throat and shook her head.

He squeezed tighter. Why was her daddy hurting her?

"Promise me now. Promise."

"Why were you kissing that lady?"

He released his tight hold and swiped a hand through his hair. "I had too many beers I guess. It was stupid, a big mistake. I promise I'll never do it again. Now you've got to keep this our little secret okay? Do I have your word?"

She had nodded, reluctantly promising to keep his dirty secret. Three months later, her dad walked out and left them both for that horrible woman.

An eternity later, Mary made her way to baggage claim. She ignored the temptation to run outside and kiss the ground. She should go straight to the ticket counter and get a flight home, but the thought of getting back on that steel bucking bronco ensured that wouldn't happen. A crowd thronged the carousel, but she managed to wiggle to the conveyor and collect her luggage. Now what? She punched David's number, and got his voicemail. A defeated sigh escaped her lips as she waited for the beep.

"David, hey it's me. I'm here but…I think I made a mistake." Out of the corner of her eye, Mary caught sight of what looked to be Santa Claus, waving a festive sign with shiny gold font, with *Mr. and Mrs. Walker* plastered on the front. Warmth crept up her cheeks. "David, I'll call you back." She slipped the phone into her pocket and hurried toward the white-bearded man, maneuvering around children distracted by Ol' Saint Nicholas.

When the man zeroed in on her, he smiled, revealing rosy dimpled cheeks. "Mrs. Walker, I presume?"

"Mary," she corrected, holding out her hand. The last person she wanted to be right now was *Mrs. Walker.*

He took her hand, his touch creating a strange tingling sensation in her fingertips. Her hand quivered as if she'd been injected with a shot with of joy.

"You can call me Nick."

She nodded and pulled her hand back.

The man looked over her shoulder. "We'll wait a moment for Mr. Walker, and then we'll be on our way."

"Oh…he's not coming." She shook her head. "He didn't make the flight."

"He'll be here, my dear." Santa's tone sounded a bit too confident.

"No. He's not coming. You see. He pulled a prank on me. It's just me. And I'm not going to be staying long. Just long enough to get over the fear of flying again."

Santa's gaze zoomed over her shoulder, and his face lit up. Mary sensed someone behind her.

21

JT.

"Sorry I'm late." JT's huge body brushed up against her as he shook Nick's hand.

Mary's knees felt a little wobbly. Mad at herself for feeling relieved. His scent circled around her in a warm familiarity. She took an involuntary whiff. Musk and soap, a simple smell unique to JT. Much nicer than the nostril burning sweetness of David's two-hundred-dollar stuff. Good Lord, why did she compare the two?

"I'm JT Walker."

"Call me Nick." Santa chuckled. "You're not late. You're right on time."

Where had JT come from? He hadn't been on the plane. "How'd you get here?"

"This friendly flight attendant bumped me up to first class." His devilish grin agitated her.

So he purposely let her fly alone, knowing she'd freak? *Jerk.*

They followed Nick toward the exit.

"Think there's a sleigh waiting outside?" JT whispered. The heat of his breath sent shivers along her spine.

"Maybe." She glanced around. "We did land in Vermont and not the North Pole, right?"

"Hope so."

Icy wintry air welcomed her at the door. "Wow. It's freezing."

JT chuckled. "I think this *is* the North Pole."

A sleigh didn't await them, but an old red-and-white pick-up truck with an evergreen wreath tied to the grill did.

"You'll get used to it." Nick bellowed out a strange laugh. Not a "ho, ho, ho," exactly, but something close.

His round belly *did* look similar to a bowl full of jelly.

Holy mistletoe. What had their mothers gotten them into?

Nick settled their luggage in the back and opened the passenger door. Mary began to climb in when Santa placed a gentle hand on her shoulder, stopping her.

No. Her frozen fingers and toes protested. She needed heat, and she needed it now.

He held up a clipboard with an attached pen. "Before we go any further, I need to get your John Hancocks on these papers, please."

"What's this?" Mary's eyes blurred from the cold, and she could barely focus.

JT grabbed the pen and signed. Then held it out for her.

"Wait. I'm not signing anything until I've had a chance to read it." David's face flashed before her. The lawyer in him would have a cow if she signed something without giving the papers her once-over.

JT jerked his collar up around his neck. "Mary, it's freezing out here. I'm sure it's the same thing you sign when you check in at a hotel." He looked to Nick for confirmation.

The man raised a finger to the side of his nose and nodded. Still, something in his expression left her feeling a bit unsettled.

Before she could protest further a gust of wind caught her scarf, exposing her bare neck to the cold. An icicle down the front of her blouse would feel warmer.

"Holy crap, give me the pen." She scratched her name on the line and climbed into the pickup's bench seat. JT nestled in beside her, too close for comfort.

Nick took his spot behind the wheel, and she had

no choice but to push even closer to JT. The cramped cab was stifling. She regretted her decision more with every passing second. She'd made a huge mistake.

"Let's be on our way." The man put the truck into drive.

The warmth of JT's breath swept against her ear as he whispered, "On Dasher, on Dancer."

Mary bit at her bottom lip to keep from laughing. She would not fall for his charming sense of humor. JT was a jerk. It would be in her best interest to remember that fact.

Was she really doing this? Some crazy Christmas story gone wrong—a nightmare.

Nick drove the truck along the snow-covered roads, leaving the busyness of the city behind them. "So glad you kids could take the time to come and visit during such an active time of year."

Mary waited for JT to tell the man he had no choice, but he didn't.

"Thanks for having us." JT leaned over her as he spoke, brushing his chest against her shoulder.

The heat radiating from his body made her squirm.

JT grinned. "From the pictures, it looks like there'd be no better place to be during the holidays." She poked him in the ribs, desperate for some personal space. He moaned and settled back into his seat, still leaving one arm resting behind her neck. She arched her back and leaned forward, determined to avoid skin-to-skin contact.

After a bit, her body ached and her neck cramped, so she surrendered. Falling back, and unfortunately landing on her soon-to-be ex-husband's hard biceps.

She should kill her mother.

Just because she had to touch him didn't mean she had to look at him. She stared straight ahead. Miles and miles of snow-capped mountains passed by. The landscape was almost too perfect. Her gaze followed a small rabbit scurrying along a field until her view was blocked by JT's profile. His expression seemed a little too cocky. *Cocky now. Miserable later.* He would hate being cooped up without his work.

Nick laughed, a quieter version of his "ho, ho, ho." "I think you'll enjoy your holiday."

Mary didn't want to enjoy anything. She pulled her phone from her pocket to glance at the time and to see if David had called her back. Zero bars. *Great. Just great.*

JT snuggled in closer. She rewarded him with another jab. He groaned, and she grinned. He'd better back off or next time she would shoot for his jingle balls.

What was he trying to pull, being so friendly? They were a couple on the brink of divorce. A month away from being strangers. A pain squeezed her heart, and a hint of tears stung the back of her eyes. Good Lord, she needed to escape the truck. And soon.

The sun settled behind the clouds, casting silver, glistening sparkles across the land. Lights of a small town shimmered in the distance.

"Is that it?" She pointed at the town before her.

Nick chuckled. "Yes, it is. That's Jollyville."

The buildings grew closer. There was something majestic about the little town setting in the middle of nowhere.

Mary couldn't believe her eyes. Jollyville resembled a Christmas town out of a Norman Rockwell painting. Buildings neatly nestled together in a large square, outlining a central park. White lights shone from every window and along the roof tops. Wreaths hung from every door and evergreen garland with huge red bows draped from one street lamp to another. The scene looked too perfect.

"Something's missing," Mary said, not sure what.

"Cars," JT announced. "Where are the cars?"

He was right. No vehicles of any kind, anywhere.

"We set up the town so all the parking would be behind the buildings. I'm only driving through town now to give you a little welcoming tour."

"It makes a huge difference," JT said.

He was right. "So I guess this town had a vision even before it was built. How old is Jollyville?"

Nick chuckled his "ho, ho, ho" laugh. "It's pretty old."

How could that be? Even though the town had a vintage appeal, it appeared fresh. New. Clean.

Nick stopped for a young couple crossing the street. Arms full of wrapped packages. They waved, and Nick waved back.

"Merry Christmas to all," he called out the window.

JT winked at her. Obviously feeling the oddness of it all, too. This place seemed too perfect to be believed.

When they approached, the Rekindle Inn appeared even lovelier than the brochure. The three-story Victorian boasted a huge wraparound porch with several sets of French doors. Candles lit every window, and garlands draped the porch rails. Lights, lights, and more lights lit every inch of trim.

Her skin tingled and her cheeks flushed. *What a*

magical sight.

Nick stopped the truck and a young man in green slacks, red coat, and a pointy hat ran down the steps. He jerked open the door for Nick.

"I'm so sorry, sir, that I wasn't here to pick up the Walkers. I got held up at the stables."

"It's fine, Norman. I didn't mind at all." Nick slipped out of his seat.

"I know you don't, sir, but you are much too busy to have to do my chores."

Chores. Mary rolled her eyes. *Okay.*

Norman ran around and reached for JT's door, but her ex-husband beat him to it. Mary all but pushed JT out of her way, in her frantic yearning for fresh air.

Norman held his hand out to her, and she accepted his assistance. He pulled, and she almost tumbled out. For a small guy, he sure was strong. "Welcome, Mr. and Mrs. Walker." He flashed them a grin, then hurried to retrieve their bags.

Could people stop calling her Mrs. Walker? She was only going to be Mrs. Walker for one more month, and then she'd go back to her maiden name.

She glanced up at the lovely, romantic inn, and her insides turned to mush. Why was she here? The trip went beyond a dare *or* to please her mother. Why didn't she stand up to her mom like she should have done years earlier?

This was all JT's fault. She had no intention of setting foot in Jollyville until he challenged her. Anger tinged the hairs on her neck. How silly to take his bait.

She should be back in Virginia at David's firm's Christmas party. *Darn.* The idea of another stuffy black-tie event crawled up her spine and smacked her in the back of the head. She hated them. She'd definitely landed in a no-win Christmas.

Mary stood stiff as a statue, feeling lost. She didn't belong with David, and she certainly didn't belong here with JT.

Norman hurried up the steps with her luggage before she had the chance to demand he put it back in the truck and return *it* and *her* to the airport.

"Mary, you coming?" JT stared back from the bottom of the steps. When she didn't answer, he hurried to her. "What's up?" He had the nerve to sound concerned.

"JT, what are we doing here?"

He shrugged. "Freezing." His jest lightened her mood, but just a little.

"No. I mean what are we really doing here? Prolonging the agony?" She crossed her hands in front of her. "I'm sorry. I shouldn't have challenged you. This isn't a game. It's our lives." She turned her glassy gaze from him. "You were right. I need to stand up to my mom. And I should have done so before I let this charade go this far."

"Hey…"

She wouldn't look at him. She couldn't.

He brushed his thumb under her chin and turned her face toward him. Their gazes locked, and so did her insides.

"I could have stopped it, too. I didn't want to." His mouth curved upward. "Mary, maybe our marriage became a disaster there at the end."

"Understatement."

"At one time, we were best friends. I don't expect this week to change anything concerning the divorce, but I'm kind of hoping we won't hate each other when we leave."

Her heart sank. She didn't want to hate him. Life would be so much easier if she could.

"Stop thinking about it as a marriage rekindling thing," he said with a nod toward the inn. "Instead, think of it as a Christmas vacation with an old friend." His lips curved up. "Who unfortunately happens to be your almost-ex."

A smile tugged at her lips, but she worried it away. She understood what JT meant, yet she still believed the trip one huge mistake.

"Have fun, Mary. You deserve it." He shot her a dimpled grin. "I promise I'll be nice. In fact, I'll stay away from you entirely if that's what you want."

"In that case I'll stay—ha, ha."

He chuckled. Then stood quietly, gazing at her with a sincere expression. He held his hand out for her.

Not good. Could she be friends with JT without letting her heart get involved again? Her inner voice screamed, *No. Run. Grab a reindeer and fly the heck out of here, while you have the chance.* It wouldn't be the first time she ignored her inner voice. She grasped the hand he offered and let him lead her up the steps.

When they'd reached the landing, Nick bellowed his good-bye from the window of his truck. They waved in return. *What a nice man—a little quirky, but nice.*

Norman guided them through the large entrance. The smell of fresh evergreen overwhelmed Mary.

Wow. The Rekindle Inn reminded her of a *Better Homes and Gardens* December edition. A magnificent chandelier hung from the vaulted ceiling in the center.

Christmas trees and garland adorned every doorway and corner.

Norman placed their luggage in front of a mahogany check-in counter and slapped a silver bell on top. "Mrs. K will be right with you." He disappeared into a large dining room.

JT leaned into her shoulder. "Do you think if I snatched his hat off, his ears would be pointed?"

Mary smirked as she looked up into his playful blue eyes. She quickly turned away. A baby grand piano sat off to one side of a huge sitting area to the left. A young girl sat at the pearly keys, playing "Silent Night." Actually, not a young girl at all but a very small woman.

JT turned toward the music, too. "North Pole it is. I suggest you be on your best behavior. You wouldn't want to end up on the naughty list." He winked, earning him a jab in the side.

"Shhh. She might hear you."

"I'd forgotten how violent you are." He grinned and rubbed his rib cage.

A blazing fire crackled from a large fireplace behind the piano. Candles illuminated every inch of the mantel, and a huge wreath hung from the wall above. Elegant Victorian furniture looked cozy and inviting. Mary fought the urge to go crawl into a chair and soak up the warmth.

She felt a tingling sensation again, as if a magical awareness had taken over her body the moment she crossed the town limits. A warm and fuzzy feeling.

Mary closed her eyes to clear her head. Her imagination had spilled over.

Get it together. Stick to the mission. She needed to

get through one week in this crazy Christmas town. Mom would be happy. And she'd be another week closer to her divorce. Freedom remained her ultimate goal, right? Salvaging a friendship with JT didn't seem possible. The last thing her broken heart needed was to be friends with the breaker

A joyful humming caused her to turn. A short, plump woman with gray hair pinned neatly in a bun had walked up behind her. *Mrs. Claus.*

The woman's hazel eyes sparkled behind wire-rimmed glasses, and her face lit up as bright as one of the many Christmas trees.

Mary didn't understand how she knew, but she recognized the lady in the red turtleneck and green plaid skirt as Nick's wife. *Yep.* Crazy-Christmas town just upgraded to *get-me-the-heck-out-of-here* nut house.

"Mr. and Mrs. Walker, what a pleasure to meet you." The woman extended her hand. "I am Mrs. Klaus…" A small giggle escaped. "With a K."

Mary nibbled on her bottom lip to keep from laughing at the ridiculousness. To say they'd gone overboard on the Christmas-North-Pole premise would be an understatement.

She didn't dare to make eye contact with JT, or she'd be done for. When she shook the woman's hand, she got the same tingly feeling as she had with Nick, but this time instead of joy, something akin to *love* flooded her senses.

She retrieved her hand. *Christmas creepy.*

"Let's step into my office." The woman waved them to a room on the other side of the counter, pulling the French doors closed behind them. She took her seat behind the desk and gestured for them to sit in the two

Queen Anne chairs.

"Excuse me one moment." Mrs. Klaus pulled a small metal box with a lock and two tiny keys from a drawer. She also retrieved a few papers and lined everything neatly in front of her with slow, graceful movements.

"I assume whoever talked you into taking this holiday, explained to you that we are not your," she arched a brow, "typical inn."

Mary glanced at JT.

"You could say that," he answered.

"Good, we don't like people to be surprised when we tell them what we do here."

Mary's jaw clenched. "Just what *do* you do here? I mean we read the brochure, and we know it's for couples that are trying to save—For couples contemplating divorce, but what exactly is involved?"

"We are about to go over all the details, Mrs. Walker." Mrs. Klaus paused. "Do you mind if I call you by your given names?"

She shook her head. JT did the same.

"Let me see." Mrs. Klaus looked at the paperwork. "Joseph and Mary? But it says here you liked to be called JT. You may call me Joy."

Back the Santa sleigh up—Joy Klaus. Too corny to be believed.

"We ask that you take this week to try and rekindle the feelings you once shared for one another. The love that brought the two of you to the altar"—she glanced at the paperwork—"almost six years ago."

Mary frowned. Should she fess up now? Tell Joy Klaus this was just a big waste of time? She didn't want the woman to go to so much trouble when their marriage teetered one judge's signature from being over.

"We ask that you partake in the activities we have planned for you," Mrs. Klaus continued.

JT sighed. "Does that include marriage counseling junk?"

Joy Klaus' expression hardened, exposing lines on her forehead. She glared at him from behind her outdated glasses. Her face relaxed. "We don't have any marriage counseling sessions. We only have winter-wonderland activities. However, we do ask that you participate in a few thinking exercises. Nothing too painful, I assure you." She shot JT a disapproving scowl. "You will have an itinerary to follow. We do require that you both commit to the schedule. It's most important."

Mary's gaze dipped to the floor, then toward JT. They should come clean now. Stop the foolishness. Maybe salvage some of the wonderland vacation Mrs. Klaus referred to—separately, of course.

Both stared in deafening silence. Neither admitted the truth.

The woman cleared her throat. "Let's get started, shall we?" She handed each of them a blank piece of paper and a pen.

"I need you to write down in a few words, what you feel has been the downfall of your marriage. What has caused you such pain that you feel it's impossible to fix?"

It didn't take long to complete the exercise. Mary jotted on her paper and handed the page to Joy. JT returned his at the same time.

Mrs. Klaus looked at each paper before turning her

warm gaze back to them.

She read aloud from Mary's paper. "Workaholic. Untrustworthy. Dishonest swine."

JT snickered.

Mrs. Klaus picked up his paper. "Lack of trust. Stubborn and refuses to listen."

Mary's cheeks warmed, and she leaned back in her chair. Not surprising JT wrote lack of trust. She didn't trust any man. Why should she?

Mrs. Klaus folded the two small pieces of paper and dropped them in a red ceramic bowl. She took a candlestick from a holder and with the flame, set the pages on fire. Mary watched the parchment turn to ash. The smoke rose upward in a twirling spiral of gray, forming a perfect heart before vaporizing into thin air.

Holy jingle bells.

She had to have imagined the heart. This place made her nuttier than a fruitcake.

Chapter 3

Mrs. Klaus looked over her glasses. "From this moment on, you shall refrain from discussing anything to do with these words. At least with each other. Any questions about that?"

"I guess it makes sense in one way," Mary said. "But if we never talk about it, how do we resolve our problems?"

Good Lord, what did she say? She'd gotten sucked in. She hadn't come there to resolve problems.

Mrs. Klaus brightened. "This week we would like to take you back to the beginning. It's about rekindling the love you once shared. The way you felt about each other when you were first married." The woman handed them what looked to be an agenda. "This is the main schedule of events. You can review it later. You will see some time allotted that reads: *one plus a guide*. That is the time when you will do things separately, with your assigned guide. The guide will be me, Mr. Klaus, or someone on staff."

"Do we ever get any time alone?" Mary asked.

Mrs. Klaus grinned and a blush dusted her cheeks. "Alone, as in the two of you alone in your room? Of course."

Mary's own blush raced to her cheeks. "No. I mean alone, alone."

"If you wish." Mrs. Klaus retrieved another paper

from her stack. "Good. I see you've signed your commitment agreement."

Mary swallowed. "What commitment agreement?"

She turned the paper toward them for review. "The form you signed at the airport. This agreement states your commitment and promise to abide by the rules and regulations of the Inn."

Mary shot JT an *I-told-you-so* glare. Wait. How in the world had the agreement ended up on Mrs. Klaus' desk?

This was too much. She needed to get out of this place now. Time to confess.

"Mrs. Klaus we appreciate everything you do here, but to be honest, we're only here because we didn't want to hurt our parents' feelings. I'm afraid we are just wasting your time."

She waited on the edge of her seat for Mrs. Klaus to tell her deceptions made her a horrible person, but instead she arched her back and delicately folded her hands in front of her.

"I understand." Her expression softened. "You are not the first couple to sit in this office and tell me it's too late. However…you both did come. That means something."

She wouldn't take no for an answer. Mary opened her mouth to protest some more but didn't get the chance.

"Besides. You both signed the commitment agreement. So, for one week you belong to the Rekindle Inn."

She held out the paper toward Mary. Unbelievable. She snatched it from her and read the stupid thing out loud.

"I agree to follow the rules and regulations of the Rekindle Inn, for the entire length of my stay. So I can devote my love, my time and myself to my spouse and the success of our marriage." She scanned further. More blah, blah, blah, basically saying the same thing.

"You can't really believe this to be binding?"

"Of course I do."

Mary felt the heat overtake her body and knew she was covered in splotches. Something that always accompanied her temper. She should call David. He would set Mrs. Klaus straight about her ridiculous commitment agreement.

Mrs. Klaus went on. "Now for the hard part. But remember you signed the agreement," she said pointing a sturdy finger at them. She opened the metal box with one of the keys hanging from the lock. "I will need your cell phones, iPods, MP3s, keys, all forms of ID, wallets, all cash, credit cards and anything else that may assist you to leave the property before your week is up." She rattled off the list so quickly it took Mary a second to recall the words.

What the...she had to be kidding?

"That seems a little extreme. What if we need money?" JT protested.

Mary glared at JT. *Finally—the mute speaks. About time.*

"You won't." Mrs. Klaus assured him. "Everything as far as entertainment, food, drinks has been paid for; any souvenirs you may wish to purchase can be charged to your room, to be satisfied at check out."

Mary couldn't contain the laugh bubbling up to her throat. The entire set-up seemed ridiculous. She shook her head and backed up in her chair. She'd kill her mother when she got her hands on her.

JT started pulling things from his pockets and tossing them in the metal box. Mary glared at him in stunned silence. He actually planned to go along with these shenanigans.

"What if there's an emergency at home?" JT asked, hesitating before handing his phone over.

"It says in your paperwork that both of your mothers know where you are. They can reach you anytime, if they feel it is important enough."

When JT dropped the last of his things in the box, all four eyes turned to Mary.

"I'm sorry. I won't do it. I'm not going to walk off the face of the earth for a week without telling someone what's going on."

Mrs. Klaus gave her an understanding frown. "I appreciate your apprehension. Our ways can come across as a little unorthodox."

You think?

"I can assure you, there's no cause for alarm. Your things will be safe."

"Mrs. Klaus, do you mind if I have a moment with JT?"

"Of course." Mrs. Klaus stood and walked to the door. "I'll be waiting outside when you are ready to continue." She disappeared behind the glass door.

Mary leaned toward JT. "What is the matter with you? This could be some sort of identity-theft ring for all we know. In a week we'll be completely wiped out."

The look he sent back screamed disappointment. "Admit it, Mary. You're chicken."

"Chicken? Don't tell me you can't see that there is something crazy about this"—she tossed flailing hands in the air—"place."

He shrugged. "It's a little weird, I admit. But what the hell do we have to lose?"

"Umm—everything."

JT frowned and tapped his knuckles on his thigh. "God, Mary, for once in your life trust someone."

This had to be a dream. No. A nightmare. Was she the only one using common sense here? "JT, this isn't about trust, this is about being logical."

"Mary. Our moms wouldn't put us in a situation that would bring us harm." He sighed, then raised a brow. "If you think about it, it makes perfect sense. The first fight, and one of us would be running for the airport." He leaned an arm across the back of his chair in a relaxed admit-I'm-right manner. "Makes sense to me."

She wanted to clobber him. Everything in her head told her to get up and leave Looneyville. But her heart kept her plastered to her seat. And that fact frightened her more than identity fraud.

Mrs. Klaus knocked gently and then entered. "Are we ready to proceed?"

They nodded. Mary pulled her belongings out of her purse and pitched them in the box. *This is not happening.*

JT and Mrs. Klaus started chatting as if they were old friends. *Crazy-town. I've stepped out of the real world and landed in North-Pole crazy-town.* And by JT's lack of suspicion, he could be a permanent resident.

Mrs. Klaus watched as Mary dropped the last of her personal things in the box. She didn't close the box, instead gave Mary a knowing stare.

Really? Did this place have a hidden camera? She retrieved the credit card she'd secretly crammed in her coat pocket and tossed it in the box.

Mrs. Klaus smiled and locked the box with the small key. She then took the box and placed it in a bigger safe behind her. She held out the smaller keys for each of them.

Ridiculous. Totally ridiculous. Mary took the key and dropped it in her pocket.

"Now you are the only ones that can get into your safe, and I am the only one that can get into mine." Mrs. Klaus got back to business. "I have given you the master schedule, and a daily schedule will accompany your morning coffee tray." She stood and pushed her chair back. "We are known for our delicious coffee. It's a wonderful way to start the day." A small giggle escaped her lips.

It's probably drugged with antidepressants. People just think they're happier here because they're being pumped with magical mocha.

They followed Mrs. Klaus out, Mary turning to look at the safe one last time. An aggravated sigh escaped her lips.

Mary's muscles began relaxing as Mrs. Klaus gave them a little tour of the inn. The place had everything they could possibly need. It had a lovely restaurant. A gift shop. Two seating areas, both with large fireplaces. The second floor had a coffee shop with a little café. The further along they went in the tour, the more Mary's guard slipped away. And that couldn't be a good thing. But she couldn't help herself. The place abounded with Christmas spirit.

As they entered the café on the second floor, the

40

heavenly smell of chocolate danced in the air. Her stomach growled, reminding her that the pack of crackers she ate on the way to the airport was long gone. The young girl working behind the counter handed them both glass mugs of hot cocoa, topped with real whipped cream, finished off with a peppermint stick. Free of charge of course. They didn't fool Mary. Nothing was free. The parents had paid dearly for it.

"How about a sugar cookie?" Mrs. Klaus said, retrieving a silver plate on the counter. "They're our specialty."

Mary's stomach spoke. She grabbed a cookie and took a bite, and her taste buds soared to sugar-fix heaven. "Oh my gosh. This is delicious." She wiped crumbs from her bottom lip with the back of her hand.

JT crammed a second cookie into his mouth, agreeing with a nod of his head.

This place seemed surreal to her and a little creepy. What if the hotel fronted for a psycho movie in the making? Once the patrons checked in, they never checked out. A chill crawled up her spine stopping with tingling hair on the back of her neck. She turned to JT for comfort and released a hopeless sigh. He sipped his cocoa and chatted with Mrs. Klaus, too busy to notice anything amiss. Yep. He'd be the first killed off in this movie for gullibility.

Mom booked this vacation. She'd never put me in danger.

Maybe she should lighten up and go with the Christmas-crazy flow.

They made their way up another set of steps leading to the third floor. Mrs. Klaus paused in front of a door in the middle of the long corridor. The room number read 1225. Weird number for the third floor, but she was getting quite used to weird.

Mary turned to JT. "You want this one or the next one?" But before he could answer, Mrs. Klaus slipped the key in the door.

"You will share this one." Mrs. Klaus' eyes sparkled and her face portrayed contentment.

No way. Mary wanted to scream, "Not on your life!" when Mrs. Klaus opened the door and waved them in. Her words were lost in her throat. Stunned speechless, she gazed upon the most amazing room she'd ever seen. At least in a hotel.

A huge living area had beautiful flowered furnishings placed neatly. A fire blazed from the large fireplace, giving the room a soft glow of warmth.

Of course it fell into the same festive magic as the rest of the town. Big beautiful tree. Garland. Wreaths. All twinkling with sparkling white lights.

Mary moved into the center of the room for a better look. She knew she beamed, but she couldn't help it. She loved all things Christmas, and she'd been sent special delivery into the middle of the holiday. Off to each side of the living area were two separate bedrooms. Mary went to the one on the right and fell even more in love.

Yep. The Rekindle Inn had sucked her into its merry madness. Stick mistletoe in her hair—she was done.

A strange sensation fell over her, and her legs became a little wobbly. She reached for the chair for balance. She closed her eyes and took slow deep breaths. What was happening?

She opened her eyes once more and tried to make

sense of it. The bedroom seemed warm and peaceful. She would be safe here. She couldn't explain how she knew, but she knew nonetheless, that no matter what transpired between her and JT, she could find security in the refuge of this room.

"Does your room have a gigantic bathroom, too?" JT asked as he rushed past her to take a look. He stuck his head out of the doorway. "Yep. Jacuzzi tub and all. You gotta see this."

She pushed past him to take a look. *Good Lord, what a huge room.*

"Look at that tub." He pointed to the monstrous bathtub. "It's like twice the size of ours at the house. No getting our legs stuck in that thing."

Her cheeks warmed at the memory. His long, thick legs crammed in with hers did have a way of shrinking a tub. She nibbled on her bottom lip as she watched in amazement at how excited he'd become over a bathtub.

"Don't get any ideas." Mary crossed her arms in front of her.

He looked up, and a wicked grin turned the corners of his mouth.

"You sure?" He tilted his chin. "We could order up some champagne and start this vacation off right."

She rolled her eyes to the ceiling and then pointed a finger to the door. "Get out of my bathroom."

JT moved toward the door but stopped in front of her. He leaned into her, and she plastered herself against the wall. He raised a forearm and rested it over her head for balance. Suddenly, they were nose to nose. His eyes narrowed and grew a shade darker.

Crap.

"You sure?" he whispered, his breath warm on her

cheek.

She tried to back away, but the wall wouldn't budge. Darn it all. She needed to do something. And pulling him in for a hot, wet kiss, wasn't the rational answer. She closed her eyes against the force of his dark blue gaze.

Her eyes flew open, and she did the only thing she could do. She punched him in the gut. Not hard. Just hard enough for him to get the point.

He moaned and backed away. "Ouch." JT rubbed his stomach. His smile danced all the way to the corners of his eyes. "If you change your mind, I'll be right over there," he said tilting his head toward the door.

Mary bit back a giggle. She would never admit that she missed his attention. Nope. She didn't miss him at all.

She watched as JT's broad frame disappeared through her bedroom door to rejoin Mrs. Klaus.

Okay. Maybe she shouldn't share this suite with JT. Her heart still thumped rapidly in her chest; she knew it was the worst idea in the world. But she'd do it anyway. As long as her bedroom door had its own lock, that is.

Mary turned to the sound of a newcomer. It appeared to be the same woman they'd seen earlier playing the piano. She stood barely four feet tall, if Mary had to guess.

"Hello, Mrs. Walker." Her voice squeaked like a mouse. "I'm Missy. I'm here to unpack your things."

"That's nice, Missy. But I can do it myself." Even though there were no things to unpack at the moment, Mary noticed as she scanned the room. As if on cue, Norman came in with her luggage in tow.

"Hello, Mrs. Walker. I'm not sure we were properly introduced. I'm Norman." He had a pleasant demeanor. "I'll be here to assist you during your vacation. Anything you need, you just call Norman." His face beamed.

"Thank you, Norman."

Mary noticed Missy's eyes divert to the floor and her cheeks flushed. She hid her grin. Seemed Missy had a little crush on Norman.

"Can I get you anything, Mrs. Walker, before I leave?" he asked.

"The only thing I need at the moment is for you to call me Mary. You, too, Missy." Mary extended a warm smile to them.

"Very well. As you wish." Norman bowed before backing out of the room. He didn't make eye contact with Missy, and if that fact upset her, she didn't let on.

Missy unzipped her bags and started to put away Mary's things.

"Missy, please don't worry about that. I can do it, I really don't mind."

Missy shot her a determined glare. "No, ma'am. It's my job. Jollyvillians are very serious about their work."

And just like that, Mary remembered she'd flown to Christmas-crazy-town.

Chapter 4

"Okay. You two get some rest. You'll need it,"
Mrs. Klaus insisted. They weren't scheduled for events
until the following morning. "Take advantage of your
down time. After today there will not be much of that."
She nodded to Norman and Missy. They followed her
to the door. "Goodnight."

Mary closed the door behind them. She turned to
stare at JT. "What in the world have our mothers gotten
us into?" She walked over to the sofa and plopped
down in the center.

JT shrugged. "I have no idea. It looks like
Christmas threw up all over this place." He picked up a
porcelain Santa sitting on an end table.

"Aren't you even a little worried?" An aggravating
knot climbed up her shoulders and took residence on
the nape of her neck. She rubbed the knot with her hand
to try and ease the muscle. "In a week we could be
wiped out."

He sat the Santa on the table. "I don't know." His
blues eyes locked with hers. "I think they just take what
they do around here seriously. As far as taking our
phones and stuff," he shrugged. "Like I said earlier,
think about how many couples would take off after the
first fight if they could."

Maybe he was right. She'd already considered
bolting at least four times. She still couldn't help but

worry. This place was strange.

JT pulled the master schedule out of his pocket and sat beside her to look it over. The weight of his body caused her to slide into him. She briefly contemplated moving over to escape his warmth, but nosiness had her leaning closer for a better look. "What does it say?"

"There are some crazy things on here."

"Like what?"

He arched a dark brow. "Tubing, ice skating." He frowned. "You gotta be kidding me?"

"What is it?"

His head fell back against the pillowed sofa. "Ornament decorating." He turned toward her. "I'm sure that'll be my favorite."

She giggled. *Ha!* Served him right for taking the stupid trip in the first place.

JT stared at the list and then at her. "No way." His eyes were as dark blue as a clear winter's night.

Look away. Don't sit and think about the warm expression in those eyes. Look away.

But she couldn't. Her gaze stayed locked on his.

His mouth opened, but the words seemed lost somewhere between them. As if he'd forgotten what he was going to say? Mary figured only a second or two had passed since JT turned toward her, but it seemed like an hour. *Don't get lost in the magic of those eyes. It will only end up in disaster.* She forced her body to move a few inches away.

"Okay, I'll gladly suffer through every agonizing second of ornament decorating to get to the next thing on the list."

Her chest tingled when his grin widened, revealing those straight, white teeth. His expressions were always so animated. Wearing his feelings like an open book. At least, most of the time. Now he looked like a fifteen-year-old boy who'd just gotten a new dirt bike for Christmas.

She'd forgotten how much she missed hanging out with her husband, being near him, listening to him. Amazing how absence and time had a way of clearing things from your mind you once cherished. Mary swallowed the awkward lump building in her throat.

Her wall was crumbling, and that wasn't acceptable. She could feel it slipping with every smile on his face, every gleam in his eye.

Run. Run now. But she sat frozen. On the comfy sofa. With its adorable reindeer Christmas pillows.

"Snowmobiling!" JT blurted, clearly unaware of the war raging inside her.

She had to stop this friendship thingy going on between them. Her heart would confuse it for something else. It already had.

She slid further away from him. Clasping a pillow to her heart. "Wow. These adventures sound kind of fun. As long as I get to do them by myself."

His gaze found hers. She could see he checked her seriousness. She put on her best game face.

Come on. Believe me.

He frowned, and moved to the edge of his seat. He tossed the paper on the coffee table. "Ha ha. Very funny," he said. "Unfortunately, I think you're stuck with me."

And that thought frightened her all the way down to her red painted toenails. She didn't want to be stuck with him. She should have stood up to her mother. She could make a list from here to the airport why spending

48

this week with him was a bad idea.

Now what?

Mary tossed the pillow aside and swiped sweaty palms on her pants. "I'm starving. I'm going to get some dinner." She stood and walked to the door.

"I'll come with you." He jumped up and followed her. JT grasped the knob before she reached it, and opened the door for her. Mary couldn't move. The floor had grabbed her by the ankles and held her hostage.

Tell him no. Insist on eating alone. She opened her mouth to demand he stop being nice to her. She had a boyfriend. *Remember David?* But she didn't say any of those things. Instead, she broke free from her bondage of fear and walked through the door.

****

JT sat motionless in the inn's restaurant watching his wife fidget like a kid with a bad report card. *Great.* He and his big bathtub challenge. She'd been like a scared rabbit ever since. Ready to bolt at the first sign of trouble. He needed to back off. Get her to relax.

"I'm glad we came."

Her gaze darted to his. She probably searched his expression to determine his sincerity. He hoped she saw it. Why not? It was the truth. He *was* glad he'd come. Maybe his motive at first had been a little misguided, more for spite than anything else, but ten minutes in and he remembered how much he missed her. The way her smile lit up her entire face. Her little body jabs to his ribs caused more humor than pain. The way she nibbled on her bottom lip when she was unsure. At this rate, she'd need a lip transplant by the time the vacation ended.

"I'm serious."

49

The corner of her mouth curved. "You say that now, but you haven't suffered through ornament decorating."

He grinned. She turned away as if he'd thrown daggers at her. Her gaze settled on the blaze burning in the fireplace.

Easy to see she fought an inward battle. She didn't want to get close to him again. JT took a swallow of his wine as he studied Mary. Did she think of dorky David? His mood darkened. Sure. She'd probably rather be at this romantic inn with him. Why waste a place like this on your ex-husband? He tipped his glass again and took another gulp. "Whatcha thinking about?"

She didn't need to answer. He knew. Mary leaned back in her chair. Her stare danced over his face. She probably debated telling him the truth. But she wouldn't. Why instigate a fight? Scary how well he still knew her.

"I was thinking it's a shame Mrs. Klaus took my phone. I would love to get a picture of you decorating an ornament to send to Kyle."

JT chuckled. He'd been right. She wouldn't tell him the truth. That was okay. He wasn't sure he really wanted to hear the declaration spoken out loud anyway. He picked up his wine glass and toasted to blank air. "To Mrs. Klaus for saving my dignity."

JT's stomach knotted when Mary smiled. How did they screw up their marriage? They used to be great. Best friends. Now they were the awkward couple trying to talk about anything but real issues.

"I can still tell him about it."

JT's hand flew over his heart. "If it will bring you joy to make ornaments with me, I will gladly surrender my man card."

A giggle escaped her lips. "Please. Bring me joy?"

"Who knows? I may be so good at ornament decorating, they ask me stay on and decorate Santa's village."

Mary rolled her eyes. "Doubt it." For a quick second, he saw something in her eyes he'd recognized from the years they shared. Just as quickly, she looked away.

One step forward, five steps back.

Mary had changed over the last six months. It wasn't the fact that she'd let her blonde hair grow longer. It wasn't the fact that she wore a different shade of lipstick. It wasn't even that she was a tad thinner. No. Her change had clearly taken place on the inside. Her spark for life had dimmed.

A knot slid down JT's throat. Divorce sure had a way of sucking the joy right out of you.

The waiter brought their food. Perfect timing. He needed a diversion from the guilt stabbing his chest.

"This place is amazing," Mary said, as she looked around the room.

JT nodded. God. He wanted to say so much. But he had to be careful not to say the wrong thing. *Damn.* This sucked. Having to analyze every word coming from his mouth? He grabbed his fork and dug in. The place had him acting so weird.

Why was he strutting around like a high school rooster? Man, he needed to pull his throbbing pants in check. What did he want to achieve anyway? Did he want to save his marriage? Was he looking to be friends with the woman who held his heart by invisible strings, pulling him in any direction she wished? Heck if he knew.

She wrapped slender fingers around the stem of her glass. A strand of long blonde hair fell over her brow, and he had to resist the urge to tuck it behind her ear. He no longer held that privilege.

The way her cheeks flushed and her chest heaved in and out indicated she remained anxious. He opened his mouth to break the weird silence about fifty times, but the words were lost somewhere before delivery.

He tried again. "This is delicious." JT took another mouthful of meatloaf.

"Yes, it is." The awkward small talk deafened.

JT jerked at his collar. The temperature in the room had to be about seventy-five, but the air between them felt more like thirty.

Mary took a sip of wine, causing his chest to lock up, as if someone punched the life right out of him. Her left ring finger was bare. Her wedding rings, gone.

He hadn't noticed before. His gut burned like he'd just chugged a giant jar of jalapeno peppers. Why was he surprised? It'd been six months. Hell, she had a boyfriend. He spun his own band around with his thumb, feeling foolish for still wearing it. This night was taking a dive fast. He ran an unsteady hand through his hair. *Do something.*

The waiter replaced his empty wine glass with a full one. JT thanked him and waited until he moved out of sight. "Have you noticed anything unusual about our waiter?"

She looked up and shook her head.

He leaned in to whisper, "You haven't noticed; besides Mr. and Mrs. Klaus, no one in this town is over five feet tall?"

Her eyes widened. "I have noticed."

He leaned back in his chair. "I really think this *is* the North Pole."

Her face lit up. *Yep.* Exactly the reaction he'd wanted. Mary soaked up Christmas like a Santa-shaped sponge.

"I'm not even sure Missy would make the height requirement for the kiddy roller coaster at the amusement park." He grinned.

Mary laughed. "She is a tiny little thing."

The uncomfortable ache in JT's chest eased.

"And she likes Norman." Mary smiled her match-maker smile.

"Oh no." His brows arched. "You leave poor Norman alone."

"Why? Missy is adorable and I bet he likes her, too. Everyone could use a little push now and then."

You think? JT fought the urge to pull her out of her chair. He'd give her a push. Right into his arms.

And out of Dorky David's.

Her shoulders relaxed. Good. He didn't want her running to Mrs. Klaus and the safe the first night.

"JT, I want to apologize for earlier."

"What for?"

Her cheeks flushed. "I didn't mean to be a witch when we first got here. It's just the entire idea of surrendering our things freaked me out. In fact, I'm still a little freaked out."

He leaned in to the table. "I understand. It's a little extreme. That's for sure." JT grinned. "When she introduced herself as Mrs. Klaus I was ready to fall on the floor."

"Not just Mrs. Klaus—Joy Klaus." Her mouth

curved. "I have to admit, I can't wait to see what they have in store for us." Her eyes displayed a small spark. "There's something enchanting here, and it takes me back to my childhood." She picked up her glass. "You know, when Christmas was still magical."

JT listened without interruption. Watching his wife talk to him like she'd done a million times before seemed…right.

"Maybe this *is* the North Pole after all." Her smile grew even wider. "Who knows, if we're lucky we may even get to see the toy factory."

JT held his wine glass to hers. "To finding the toy factory."

She tapped her glass against his. He stared into her baby blues and found himself feeling very thankful for his nosy mother.

****

Past midnight and Mary couldn't sleep. Partly because of the man lying in the next room and partly due to the constant nagging feeling the trip would end in disaster. Maybe her house was being broken into this very minute. Or maybe her bank account was being wiped out. She jerked the covers around to try and get settled, but it was a waste of time. *Ohh.* She was going crazy.

She punched her pillow to fluff it. Her head plopped back down. *Nope. No better.* He still wore his wedding ring. Who did that? Good lord, it had been months. Aggravation smothered her as she stared at the ceiling.

Mary needed to get her mind off the stupid thoughts. But what could she do? Naturally, televisions were nonexistent in Santa land.

Wait.

A shelf in the living room held books. Reading would get her mind off *vacation-catastrophe*. She jerked the covers off and slid into her slippers. Mary tiptoed to the door, doing her best to be as quiet as a mouse as she unlocked the door.

She almost jumped out of her Santa-covered jammies when she saw JT leaning against the mantel. He wore striped pajama pants, minus a shirt. Every glorious muscle reflected the firelight. He hadn't heard her enter, his attention intent on the flames.

She tried to ignore how the cotton pants hugged snugly against his bottom. His dark hair moist from a recent shower. The smell of soap and musk engulfed the room. As much as she tried to stop it, the memory of sliding her fingers over every inch of his body ignited her own fire.

Look away. Just look away.

But she didn't. Couldn't.

She leaned against the door frame and wondered what had his thoughts so far away. He turned and her cheeks warmed.

Busted.

A soft smile brushed his lips. "I was thinking about our first date."

Had he read her mind again? He used to be pretty good at it.

"I had you over to my crappy little apartment for dinner. The only good thing about that dump was the fireplace."

"You cooked spaghetti."

"Yep. My famous spaghetti." He chuckled. "Remember, we started making out and I burned the garlic bread."

She grinned. "I'd forgotten about that."

"Not me. I remember every single thing about that night. I can still remember what you wore."

"Really?" Surprised, Mary walked over and sat in the flower-covered chair facing the fireplace.

He crossed his arms over his chest.

No. No. No. Ignore the bulging biceps.

"Yep. You had on a white low-cut sweater, a black skirt, and black boots. Drove me freaking insane."

Mary nibbled on her bottom lip, remembering the night. She fell in love that night. She hadn't known him long, but she knew she wanted to spend the rest of her life with him.

How did they go from there to the horrible place they were now? She pulled her knees to her chest, clutching her hands around them.

Mary knew perfectly well, how. He put his career above everything else in the world. Even her.

Especially her.

Tears burned the back of her eyes. No man voluntarily worked so much, unless the job came with fringe benefits. And even though she could never prove it, she'd bet Whitney Conner had to be his year-end bonus.

For the last two years of her marriage, she tried to ignore the hopeless feelings of being neglected, but after a while, it was all she could think about. So their marriage died a slow, miserable death. JT ditching the anniversary trip for work took matrimony's final breath.

Pain clawed at her heart as the memory of standing at the airport gate alone resurfaced. Something in her heart had died there, and nothing, including the

Rekindle Inn, could resuscitate it.

JT backed away from the fireplace and muttered something, but she missed it. Too caught up in her grief to pay proper attention. JT had clearly picked up on the chill her thoughts brought to the room, because he walked away.

A moment later his door closed behind him.

Good.

The quicker JT realized the trip figured as nothing more than obedience to their mothers' ridiculous Christmas wish, the better.

Chapter 5

Mary pulled the covers over her face the next morning to block the sun beaming through her bedroom window. She contemplated staying in bed all day, but the commitment agreement flashed in her mind. She should tell Mrs. Klaus exactly what she could do with her stupid agreement. What could the woman do? Sue her?

Mary sighed in frustration as her mood softened. Mrs. Klaus and Jollyville went through a lot of trouble to save marriages. Not their fault Mary's union with JT had run its course. Deader than last year's Christmas tree.

She leaned on her elbows. Besides, sitting in her room loathing JT wouldn't solve her problems. She slid her legs over the side of the bed and stretched her arms over her head.

Fine.

She would go along with the silly events, but it didn't mean she had to be nice to her husband—ex-husband. She made her way to the shower hoping to wash away her horrible mood, trying to ignore the wondering excitement about what this crazy little town had in store for her.

After steaming for a good twenty minutes, Mary dressed and walked in to the living room. JT hovered over the dinette table where the coffee tray had been delivered as promised. He looked huge in his flannel shirt and jeans, holding a dainty silver coffee pitcher in his large hands. He nailed the rugged lumberjack look. David, not so much.

A shiny card sat on the tray. She walked over for a better look.

JT turned. "Hey. Didn't hear you come in."

She couldn't read his tone but managed a half grin.

The card's beauty drew her attention. She rubbed a gentle finger across the word *Memory* embossed in gold lettering. Silk red ribbon trimmed the edges and the paper smelled of cinnamon.

What else would one expect from the North Pole?

JT handed her a cup of coffee.

"Thank you." She took the white holly-trimmed china and brought it to her lips. *Perfect.* Just the way she liked it. *Darn it.* Her I'm-not-going-to-be-nice-to-him shield slipped away with every delicious sip. Maybe the inn did lace their coffee with happy pills. Sure would explain why they were still in business.

Mary scanned the daily schedule. "Looks like we start with breakfast from 8:30 to 9:15, then we meet at the town Christmas tree, for…yes." She waved the card obnoxiously in front of him. "You're going to *love* this." She shot him her best sorry-for-your-bad-luck smile. "Then we go to the recreation center for…ornament decorating!" She enjoyed the agony flashing across JT's face way too much.

Served him right. Agreeing to go on the stupid trip just to spite her. She hoped he hated every second of *ornament decorating*. Her basking glory didn't last long.

"Great, may as well get it behind us," JT said, with

an unaffected shrug.

Urrgh. Not the response she hoped for. Mary slid in a chair and read more. Her eyes widened. "It says here we do the event with our plus-ones." The guides.

Yes. *Merry Christmas to me.* At least she'd get a little reprieve from JT and his overpowering dimples. Even if it meant missing out on his craft-making misery.

"Really? I thought we'd do this one together."

"Me too." She kept reading. *Darn.* "We do meet again later for a sleigh-ride luncheon at noon." *Great.* One activity that actually excited her. Why couldn't she do that with her plus-one? Any *one* but him. She'd dreamed about riding in a horse-driven sleigh her whole life.

She tossed the card back on the tray. *Oh well.* She'd make the best of the ride anyway. She refused to let JT steal that dream from her.

"Interesting." JT grunted.

Her lips twisted as she tried to read his mind. No luck. Great. Breakfast *and* lunch spent with lumberjack man. This should be fun.

Not.

****

Freezing air stole Mary's breath when she stepped onto the inn's large porch at precisely a quarter past nine. Her eyes scanned the little Christmas village surrounding her. *Surreal.* As if she stood on a stage set from a holiday movie. The townspeople were dressed in bright Christmas colors. Everyone pleasant, smiling, waving. Jollyville looked positively magical.

"Wow! It's pretty cold out here," JT said, coming up behind her. He rubbed his hands together and looked up at the sky. "Sun's nice and bright, though. It shouldn't be too unbearable."

They walked on the snow-covered sidewalk in silence, the only sound the crunching beneath their feet. *Yay.* More awkward silence. Breakfast had been bad enough. Another reminder that they'd been best friends who'd become strangers in such a short time.

Mary heard music. She stopped to listen. *No. Not music. Singing?* She glanced around. A group of carolers, bellowed out "Jingle Bells" from the corner.

"Little early in the morning for caroling, don't you think?" JT asked.

She relaxed as the Christmas spirit tingled throughout her body. "Not for the North Pole." With every step Mary took, she became...happier. As if the air cleared her head of darkness and only left the light.

JT stuffed his hands in his coat pockets. "This place is so festive. How much you want to bet we see Santa and his flying reindeer before we leave?" His eyes lit with mischief.

She laughed. She couldn't help it. Not just a giggle, a full-blown belly laugh. It must have been contagious, because JT joined her.

Good heavens, the people walking by must think they'd lost their minds. She swiped at the joyful tears running down her cheeks. What was so funny? Why couldn't she stop laughing?

"Oh my gosh, I think we've been hypnotized by magical fairy dust or something."

He laughed harder. "They must have slipped it into the scrambled eggs."

"It's magic mocha, I tell you."

Mary stopped and sucked in a deep breath. *Okay.*

Pull yourself together. What about this place made it almost impossible to be in a bad mood?

"You okay?" JT placed a hand on her shoulder.

"Yeah. I think so." She started walking again. "This place makes me feel all tingly inside." She waited for him to tease her, but he didn't.

"I know, right?" He stretched out his arms. "Like all the joy you've been holding inside for months can't help but come out."

Mary's eyes widened. "Yes. Just like that."

They walked the rest of the way in silence. Not uncomfortable silence like before, more like peaceful silence. They waited at the huge Christmas tree in the park as directed. Mary covered her cold nose with her scarf and peeked over the edge for a sign of their *plus ones*. JT grabbed her gloved hand and brought it to his lips. The warmth of his kiss pulsed all the way through to her fingers. What in the name of Santa Claus did he think he was doing?

"Thanks for coming, Mary. We're going to salvage a friendship out of this. Just wait and see."

She pulled her hand away.

Doubt it.

He must have misunderstood their sidewalk shenanigans as a sign of something more. Like she'd let him back in. But she hadn't. She couldn't. He came across as caring, but she knew better. JT only cared about one thing. Work. And he could care less if they were friends in the end. *Don't fall for it.*

"Well, good morning, Mr. and Mrs. Walker."

Mary jerked. Joy and Nick Klaus stood behind her joined arm in arm. Where the heck had they come from?

"Mary and Joseph...JT," Mrs. Klaus corrected. "I believe you've met my husband."

They nodded. JT shook Nick's hand.

"Are you ready to begin your day of *Memory*?" Nick asked, ending with his ho-ho-ho chuckle.

"I guess," Mary answered.

"Well, then say your goodbyes for now, and we'll be on our way."

JT leaned in and gave Mary an awkward hug. "See you later," he said against her ear.

"Unfortunately," she whispered back. "Have fun with your ornament decorating. If only I had my phone."

He winked. "But you don't."

Stupid commitment agreement.

****

The recreation center was a small building sitting on the edge of town. Long tables lined the room with enough decorating supplies to make a thousand ornaments. Other than craft materials, the place stood deserted. Where were all the other couples?

"Will JT be making his ornament here, too?"

"No, my dear. He and Mr. Klaus will be in another building."

A little ridiculous, considering the overkill of supplies. One more thing to add to the ever growing weird list. Mrs. Klaus led her to a table and gestured to a metal folding chair.

"Now Mary, as you know, today's magical word is *Memory*. I want you to think back. Is there a special memory you have of Joseph? One that helped convince you, you couldn't live without him?"

Why go there?

Mrs. Klaus pursed her lips and raised her brows.

Mary straightened in her chair. *Great.* Could she read minds, too? "Mrs. Klaus, that's a tall order. It's been quite a while since I've recalled any memories like those."

Joy folded her hands on her round belly. "I'm sure you have many. You must clear your mind of the recent clutter and think back to the beginning."

Recent clutter? Is that what you call months of misery?

Mary relaxed into her chair. She released a long sigh. *If I must.* She pushed aside the pain of the last year and returned to the beginning of their relationship. The memory surfaced right away. *Wow. Who would have thought?*

"I see by the gleam in your eyes you've remembered something special."

Mary stared at the holly-print tablecloth.

"Yes. I guess I have." Her gaze locked with her companion's. "JT and I had been dating for a little over a year. It was Christmas Eve, and I was upstairs in my room. I still lived at home with my mom." Not because she couldn't afford her own place, but because she'd been afraid to leave her mother in the house all alone. "Anyway, I was lying across my bed, thinking how deeply I loved him." Her jaw tightened. "I wanted so desperately to believe in our mutual love...but—" The words froze in her throat.

"But with your father walking out on you and your mother, you found yourself doubting."

Mary jumped to attention. "Yes. How did you...?" She shook her head trying to make sense of Mrs. Klaus' words. *Bizarre. Plain bizarre.*

"I guess you could say I had a hard time trusting happiness." Mary wrung her fingers together. "You see, my parents seemed to be so in love, so it came as quite a shock when my father came home one day and told mom he wanted a divorce. He said he never really loved her at all, and he'd finally fallen in love for the first time, with someone else." Mary shook her head, loathing the memory.

"Anyway, naturally I wanted to believe in the love JT and I shared, but I was scared to death. A thousand doubts ran through my head that day." Her lashes were wet with tears. "What if JT only thought he loved me?"

Mrs. Klaus didn't say anything.

"Anyway, as I laid there contemplating my life, I heard a clink on my bedroom window. I looked out and there was…" Mary swallowed the lump in her throat, trying to finish the story without breaking down.

Where was the magic mocha when she needed it? Mrs. Klaus waited patiently.

"JT was parked out front, leaning against his truck. He held up a sign that said *I love you.* Then he flipped to another one: *Let me be your hero.*" She dissolved into tears. Waterworks. She hated waterworks. She swiped her fingers over her face.

"Then he flipped another one: *Marry me.*"

She sniffled. Mrs. Klaus handed her a handkerchief. She wiped her face, then held the white linen fabric in her lap. Her finger traced over a beautiful green Christmas tree embroidered on the corner, then touched the red ribbon outlining the edges. *Of course.* The North Pole wouldn't have paper tissues like the rest of the world.

She took a moment to pull herself together. When

she found her voice again, a small smile fanned her lips. "That is my favorite memory."

"It's indeed a lovely memory." Mrs. Klaus patted Mary's hands.

"Of course JT doesn't do things like normal guys with the bended knee and fancy dinner." Like David would surely do. "JT's always been his own guy." Her mood lightened. "I guess it's one of the things I love about him most." Her eyes opened wide. "Loved. Loved about him."

Geez. This place really had gotten to her.

Mrs. Klaus stood. "Now I'm sure we can find some things around here to make an ornament to represent such a special memory."

Mary joined her and they walked around the room, gathering supplies. Then they went straight to work.

****

JT wanted to tell Nick making an ornament had to be the corniest thing he'd ever done, but he figured the exercise would take only a couple of hours of his life. Plus, he was hundreds of miles away from the guys. No one would ever find out.

Nick explained the *memory* concept. JT rummaged through his past. "Wow. This is going to take a second." He rubbed a hand over his chin. There were so many times she'd done great things for him, he had a hard time narrowing them down.

Then he shot Nick his poster boy smile. He had it. Settling back in his chair, he crossed an ankle over his knee. "We'd only been going out about seven months. I was supposed to attend this black tie presentation at Mary's publishing firm." He shook his head. "On a Saturday in the middle of the day." *What idiot made that schedule?* "But man I didn't want to. I fit in at a black tie event like the Abominable Snowman would fit in at the North Pole."

"Well, actually he does…" Nick shook his head. "Never mind. Go on with your memory."

JT tilted his head to the side. *Okay.* "I wanted to go by the job site to check on things, and I really needed to go by the supply store." JT frowned. "Well, to be honest, I guess I wanted to do just about anything on a Saturday but go to the event."

"I see." Nick's tone sounded flat.

JT rubbed his neck. "God, talk about stupid."

"We've all been stupid a time or two," Nick interjected with a raised brow.

"I called Mary and told her I really needed to work, and of course being the angel she is"—*or was*—"she bought my lame excuse. She told me not to worry, there'd be plenty of other events. I didn't know she'd been nominated for assistant editor of the year, and my dumb ass wasn't there when she won."

Yikes. The reasons for the fall of his marriage became more clear with every word.

"And this is your *favorite* memory?" Nick tapped his chubby knuckles on the table.

"I'm getting to that part," JT said, with a thin smile. "I did go by the job site, but I don't even think I got out of my truck. My buddy Kyle was there and suggested we take the dirt bikes out." He raised a brow. "And we did."

JT shook his head. "Well, I went out riding and in my attempt to imitate the great Jeremy McGrath, I took a jump my amateur skills couldn't handle. I came down and rolled with the bike about three times. I broke my ulna and my radius." He slid his finger along his arm to show the location.

Nick laughed. "I keep waiting for the happy story here, but it only gets worse."

"It's coming. I promise. Anyway, I figured I'd screwed up with Mary. I'd lied about working and I was going to be caught red-handed." JT straightened in his chair and crossed his arms over his chest. "But Mary didn't get angry, instead she worried about me getting hurt. She rushed to the hospital and stayed by my side until they released me. I had a cast from the top of my right arm to the tip of my fingers. What a pain in the butt. Let me tell you, being right handed, that sucked." JT shrugged his shoulders.

"Well, being the independent he-man I am, I didn't want someone doing things for me, but Mary insisted. She handled all my cleaning. She cooked for me and did my laundry. I had a Mustang back then, too, with a manual tranny. Mary drove around with me and shifted the gears, while I steered with my left hand."

Wow. She loved him so much back then. JT's stomach knotted. How had he turned such a love against himself in such a short time?

Nick didn't interrupt. Clearly still anticipating the happy ending.

"I guess this may seem like a pathetic story to you, but the accident became a valuable lesson for me." He folded his hands in his lap. "I found my angel on earth. Someone to cherish. Mary was the most kind-hearted, unselfish person I'd ever met. I fell in love with my angel then, and I fell hard." He smirked. "I knew I needed to make that girl my wife before I did something else stupid and lost her for good."

Nick chuckled. "So you're saying, it took a broken arm to make you see the light?"

"Yep. I guess it did."

Nick glanced around the room. "I'm sure we can come up with something." And they did. Once the ornament dried they placed it in a small red gift box. JT spent the time fighting the bitterness eating away at his gut. Bitterness toward himself. He'd sworn then he'd never do anything stupid again that could cause him to lose Mary. Yet he'd gone and done exactly that. He put work first and her last.

Dumb-ass.

Chapter 6

Mary walked out of the recreation center two hours later, with a small wrapped box tucked in her coat pocket. She wasn't sure what to do with it now. Mrs. Klaus said she'd tell her when the time came.

Joy Klaus hummed alongside her.

"We have a little time before we need to have you back at the park. How about a cup of cocoa at the Peppermint Cafe?"

Mary was freezing. "Sounds wonderful."

As they walked the block and a half to the eatery, she remained in awe of Jollyville's vintage beauty. Park activity flourished. People walked the streets. Boys were having snowball fights. Children laughed as they made snow angels. The sound warmed Mary's heart. Two men stretched on ladders around the huge Christmas tree, hanging lights. Parents watched their children play.

"Mary, I'm so glad you and JT came to stay with us."

"Thanks." She walked a few steps. "Mrs. Klaus. I still feel we are wasting all these lovely resources you could be sharing with couples who haven't quite given up."

Mrs. Klaus clasped her hands behind her back. "I'm sorry you've given up on your marriage, Mary."

A ping of guilt pinched her heart.

"We've helped many a couple over the years who were sure they were doomed. But somehow they worked things out."

"But for how long?" Mary folded her arms together. "Maybe they get swept up in this magical place and the illusion of happiness, then find when they get home, all the problems come right back."

Mrs. Klaus gestured her to the entrance of the café. They went inside and made themselves comfortable in a large booth.

A redhead with matching neon lipstick and a shiny gold apron, waved cheerfully from behind the counter. Her smile revealed a slight overbite. "Hey, Mrs. K. I'll be right with y'all."

"Take your time, Deloris."

Hey, wait a minute. Deloris was at least five foot seven. Mary hid a frown. There went her and JT's North Pole elf theory.

She looked up to find Mrs. Klaus staring at her. "You may not believe this, my dear, but every couple who came to the inn and followed our unusual rules are very happily married today."

Mary leaned back against the red cushioned seat. *No.* There was no way she'd believed such a thing. How in the world could Mrs. Klaus know?

Deloris set two cups of cocoa in front of them.

Mary glanced toward her. "Thank you."

"No problem, Mrs. Walker. Enjoy."

How did Deloris know her name?

The woman gave Mary the once-over as she smacked a cheek full of gum. Her sympathetic stare didn't go unnoticed. "Hope you're enjoying your stay in Jollyville."

"Yes. It's lovely."

The rush of heat raced to Mary's face. God, did everyone in this town know she and JT were a pathetic loser couple?

"Hope you and Mr. Walker find your way over here for dinner sometime. We have the best chicken and dumplings in the entire northern hemisphere."

"Wow." *Way to be modest.*

Deloris fidgeted with her apron. "Anyhow. You bring your hunky husband in here to see us, you hear?"

"Thank you, Deloris. That will be all for now." Mrs. Klaus dismissed her like an employee rather than a café owner. Deloris gave a nod before moving behind the counter.

Joy took her spoon, swiped a big glob of whipped cream from the top of her cocoa, and stuck it in her mouth. "Now where were we?" She pursed her lips. "Oh yes. You were wondering how we know our couples are still together."

What in the world? Mary hadn't expressed her doubt out loud.

"We receive the nicest Christmas cards every year from all of our former guests. Most have added little elves to their families." She giggled. "Oh, the beautiful babies." Her gaze softened. "When I think of all those precious babies that wouldn't have been born if the parents hadn't given love another try."

Mary's heart raced. Mrs. Klaus couldn't take the credit for all the babies. Maybe if the couples divorced, they would have met other people and had children. At least it's what she'd like to believe. Had to believe. She held on to the dream of having her own children one day. Tears threatened to spill.

She wouldn't cry. And she wouldn't think about how cute JT's babies could be. *Nope.* She'd done it a thousand times during her marriage. And she definitely wouldn't think about JT having children with someone else.

Mrs. Klaus reached over and laid her hand across hers. A tingling warmth overcame her.

Whoosh.

The tears and negativity disappeared. Just like that.

Okay. Change the subject. "So you have a one-hundred-percent success record?" Then it dawned on her. Good grief. They would be the first couple to ruin Christmas in Jollyville. Talk about a cup of hot cocoa with a side of guilt.

"No. I wish I could say such a thing."

Then what the heck did Mrs. Klaus just say?

"There was one couple who didn't make it." Grief swept over Joy's face. "Let's just say the husband made your skepticism seem like a single snowflake in a raging winter storm."

Mary blushed. "Come on, Mrs. K; in my defense, you've got to admit this whole idea is a little unorthodox."

Mrs. Klaus, giggled again. "I suppose." She folded her hands in front of her, and her mouth set in a soft line. "This couple left after the second day. If only they would have given us a chance."

"I didn't know you could leave?"

The older woman's eyes grew large. "Good Lord, child, we haven't kidnapped you." She arched one brow. "You are free to leave anytime you'd like." She placed her hand on Mary's arm. "But please don't leave before giving us a chance to help you."

"But the agreement. The safe with the lock?"

"We do the lockbox, so people don't run off in a fit of anger or hurt. You'd be surprised how much a person can simmer down by the time they get the three key holders together."

Now *that* Mary could live with. Made perfect sense. The hostage premise stunk.

"Unfortunately, his anger held too long. I know we could have saved them if only we'd had more time." Mrs. Klaus frowned. "We usually are right about these things."

"I'm sure after two days it would be impossible to know."

"They were only *here* for two days; we've known them their entire lives."

"Family friends?"

"No." She winked. "We have our ways."

And just like that, they were back to *Christmas cray-cray*.

****

JT couldn't keep his gaze off Mary. She looked beautiful standing next to the park's Christmas tree. Her long blonde hair gleamed like a burst of sunshine falling around her shoulders. Pink dusted her nose and cheeks from the cold. She looked up at the sound of his crunching footsteps.

"You survived. Was it as bad as you'd imagined?" She smiled.

He'd missed her smile. Her mood seemed light. "Not bad at all. Once I got past the creepy feeling I was hanging out with the jolly-old-fat-man, himself. Always afraid I'd say or do something naughty and risk losing out on the big present drop next week."

Mary giggled. *Wow.* Had he actually made her laugh?

"Well, it doesn't really matter. There's nothing you can do to get off the naughty list anyway." Her eyes gleamed with mischief.

"I can show you naughty, if you want me to," he said, raising his brows. Oh how he wanted to. He took a step closer, but she took a step back.

"That's okay. I've seen your version of naughty. I'll pass."

"There you go being chicken again."

Her smile widened, and she rolled her pretty blue eyes. This rekindling thing wasn't half bad. He actually enjoyed teasing his wife. Who knew?

They hadn't stood together long when bustling sounded from the snow-covered hill. A sleigh pulled by two huge white horses came to a stop beside them.

Norman handled the reins. "Good afternoon, folks. Ready for your next adventure?"

JT turned to Mary and for the first time since they'd arrived, saw a change in her expression. She looked happy. Satisfaction filled him. He offered a hand and helped her climb the carriage steps. Then, he nestled in beside her. He reached for the folded quilt placed on the seat and covered their laps.

"Now this is a dream come true." Mary laughed, and the glorious sound echoed in JT's ears. He wrapped an arm around her, pulling her close. He waited for a swift elbow to the ribs, but surprisingly, she melted in beside him. Probably for warmth, but he'd take what he could get. Then, they were off. The horses' harness bells jingled in the wind as they galloped.

Norman drove the horses out of town and gave

them an amazing tour of the countryside. White-covered mountaintops cascaded in the distance. Trees blanketed in snow outlined the valleys. He admired the earth's natural beauty. The glorious vista trumped any picture he'd ever seen.

"Happy?" Her question startled him. He found her blue eyes staring at him.

"Very. You?"

"Yes. It's more beautiful than I could have ever imagined. There's something about this place that makes it almost impossible to be mad or sad." Her dark lashes lowered over her cheeks. "Maybe we can find some sort of friendship after all."

"Hope so, Mary." He placed a gentle kiss on the top of her head.

The horses came to a stop outside a little stone bungalow with smoke billowing from the chimney. Norman led them into the cozy dwelling; the warmth of a blazing fire greeted their frozen bodies. JT's nose had gone numb about a half-hour earlier.

He took a quick survey of the one-room cabin. No bed, but a couch. *Yep.* He could deal with a couch if things progressed as he'd hoped. Two chairs and a table loaded with food stood near the fireplace. He hadn't noticed any other tracks in the snow. How did the staff pull off prepping the cabin for guests?

"Wow, the fire feels good." Mary held her hands over the flames.

He moved next to her and whispered, "Did you see any tracks in the snow? Santa must have landed on the roof to get the fire started and leave the food."

Her head turned slowly. She shot him a wow-that's-a-little-creepy stare.

"Dun, dun, dun, dunt."

Mary jabbed him in the side. "Stop. You're freaking me out." Her smile contradicted her words.

Norman uncovered the silver platters arrayed on the table to reveal their lunch. He filled the wine glasses and then reached in his pocket. He stroked a match and lit the candle in the center of the table.

"All right folks. I'm out." He fist bumped JT, and then made his way toward the door. "I'll be back promptly in one hour."

An icy draft swirled around them as he left. They stood silently as the bells on the horses faded away in the distance.

"Did you teach him to fist bump?"

"Yep."

"Good grief."

An hour. He had an hour.

JT shuffled ideas about all the things he could do to Mary in an hour. *Slow down, big boy. Don't want to send her running back to the inn.*

They slid out of their coats and made a pile of gloves, scarves and hats on the side table. JT pulled a chair out for Mary, then slid into his own. She sipped at her wine and gazed into the candlelight. "I don't want to jinx it, but so far, this hasn't been so horrible."

"You're right. I guess I had all these visions of sitting in a stuffy office listening to some old guy with glasses tell us the *how-to's* of a perfect marriage."

She laughed. "I know, I sort of imagined the same thing. However, this could be a trick to get us to let our guard down. This is only our first full day."

He leaned against his chair and let the wine warm him. She was right. This was only the beginning. He had six more days to make her forget about Dorky Dave back in Virginia.

The delicious lunch did wonders filling his empty gut, but now he hoped for dessert. And not the trayful of sweet pastries arrayed next to the coffeemaker. According to his calculations, he had about twenty minutes before Norman came back to retrieve them. He could do a lot in twenty minutes. Like rocking naked around the Christmas tree.

****

Mary stood mesmerized in front of the fire. As much as she wished her mind would stop spinning ridiculous ideas of reconciliation, it taunted her unmercifully. *Your JT ship has sailed. You have a boyfriend waiting for you. Stop it. Just stop it.*

He'd been so sweet during lunch. Amazing how different he could be away from work. In fact, he hadn't mentioned his job once. *Dang.* Had to be a record.

There you go again. He's a jerk, remember?

Mary sensed when he came up behind her. Her JT radar remained on high alert. Why had she stayed so attuned to him? She turned when the warmth of his body touched hers. He glanced at the ceiling and her gaze followed. They stood directly under a ball of mistletoe.

Really, the staff couldn't have placed it better if they wanted to. *Well played, Rekindle Inn. Well played.* Before she knew his intentions, JT pulled her into his arms. His full mouth on hers.

Oh crap.

His lips were warm and tasted of wine. His kiss began soft and gentle. Then he teased her with his tongue, and she lost track of common sense. His hand slid into the back of her hair and brought her in even closer. She didn't resist him. Instead, she surrendered. Their kiss grew hotter. Scalding. Passion joined them, and she didn't try to stop the spiraling heat. They didn't kiss like this. This was like first love *oh-my-God,* inconceivably good.

The warmth of his lips tingled every inch of her body, sizzling to her core. Her body said *yes, yes,* but her brain insisted she'd jumped aboard the *you've lost your darn mind* heartbreak train. Destination: Stupidville.

Even so, Mary wanted more. More of his heat. More of his firm hold. More of him. A moan escaped her throat. Good heavens, why didn't her body just shout to the world, *I haven't been laid in six months.*

What the heck was she doing?

Friendship. Friendship was the goal.

Friends sure didn't kiss like this. She needed to stop, but God it was so good. No. She had to stop. His hand slid down her back and landed on her bottom. *Holy Christmas tree.*

Stop. Stop. Stop.

Mary put her hands on his chest and shoved. Her body hated her, but her heart would thank her later. They broke apart. She missed his warmth instantly. JT stared at her with heated eyes. But he didn't grab for her. He just let her go.

She was surprised he'd given up so easily. Did that leave her relieved or hurt? Did she want to know?

Darn this ridiculous Christmas present. She crossed her arms in front of her. Shielding her vulnerability. "What are you doing?"

JT brushed a hand through his dark hair. "I'm

sorry, Mary." His gaze went to the floor. "I guess I got caught up in the moment."

"I'd say. What the heck?" She turned her back to him. "I believe we were shooting for friendship." Her heart pounded in her ears. She wouldn't dare admit she could've stopped him the second his lips touched hers. She was partly to blame.

No. JT started the kiss, not her.

She finger-combed her hair. *Think Mary. Think.*

She had to go. She needed to leave. To get as far away from Jollyville as she could. The place made her crazy.

"I'm done. I'm not doing this anymore. I can't go through this a second time. I'm getting the key when we get back." She rubbed a hand on the back of her tensed neck. "I quit."

"Of course you do. Isn't that what you do, Mary? Quit?"

She jerked around to face him.

"When your job at East Wick got too challenging, you quit. When you went back to school for your masters, it got hard and you quit." He propped his hands on the sides of his waist. "When you get scared and think you may get hurt or fail, you quit before you get the chance to find out." JT's words were pushed from between clenched teeth.

His words acted as a sword, ripping her heart in two.

"When our marriage got a little complicated, you quit on us, too." His eyes darkened, his tone harsh. "When I met you, I would have never guessed you for a quitter."

JT's gaze turned to the ceiling, and a heavy sigh

escaped his chest. "You used to be so strong, determined." He lowered his eyes and his stare locked with hers. "What happened to that girl? Did you quit on her, too?" He rushed to the table and slung on his jacket. Then, he rushed out the door, slamming it behind him.

Her heart shattered into a thousand pieces. He'd never spoken to her like that before. He thought her a loser. A quitter. *Oh my God.* She grasped at the hurt piercing her chest. The pain was back. The excruciating pain had returned. She collapsed to her knees. All the months of healing were shattered in a matter of seconds.

****

When Norman pulled the horses to a stop in the park a half hour later, JT broke the excruciating silence.

"If you want my key, you'll have to wait for it." His tone matched the temperature outside. He climbed from the sleigh and headed toward town, his gait strong and hurried.

She sat alone in the sleigh. Unable to move. Watching him walk away. Reliving the same scene from six months earlier. Hurt and confusion burned her belly like the hot embers of a fierce wildfire.

She brushed the tears from her cheeks. *Don't let him confuse you.* What did she have to be confused about? She had a boyfriend waiting for her. One she'd recently found to be a little hot tempered and whiny, but nonetheless, a good man. She forced her eyes away from JT. Hopefully by morning she'd be back in Virginia and this stupid crazy town would be nothing but a bad memory.

An hour later, Mary had her bags packed and

sitting by the door of her room. Unfortunately, there was no sign of JT and his key. She'd also been told Mrs. Klaus had left town for the afternoon. *Yeah. Right.* Joy Klaus was *always* around. With only one key out of three, she was screwed. At least for a few hours.

Now what? How long would he make her wait for his key?

****

Mary'd been sitting on the sofa staring at the fire for two hours and still no sign of her key holders. She rubbed her tense neck. Her body ached from stress. "I can't just sit here. I'll drive myself crazy." She whispered to the empty room. What to do? What to do? Her mind drifted to the line of adorable shops on Main Street. The shops she would now miss shopping in, thanks to JT's stupid mistletoe trick. She jumped up and started pacing back and forth. The annoying clock ticked loudly on the wall, reminding her of every second she wasted sitting there pouting.

She could go shopping. Heck, why not? *Shopping makes everything better.*

Chapter 7

Sweat poured from JT's brows as he used every drop of energy to lift the weighted bar over his chest. His arms shook, but he managed to boost the bar high enough to send it slamming into the holders with a loud clunk. He really should've had a spotter, but his temper insisted he do it alone.

He laid on the bench in complete exhaustion.

"Feel better?" Nick stood to the side watching him. He wore a corny red sweat suit with a matching headband.

JT grinned. He couldn't help it.

"Not really."

Nick's ho-ho-ho caused his large belly to giggle.

Must be his first time in the Jingle It All Away Gym. JT sat up and swiped a towel across his face.

"You'll find the gym to be your best friend this week," Nick said, picking up a five pound dumbbell and bending his elbow back and forth. He'd definitely shown up for the pep talk and not the burn.

"Yep. I imagine so." JT was cooked. He couldn't lift one more ounce.

"How was the horse-drawn sleigh ride?"

"Good. Good."

"How about lunch? Great little cottage isn't it?"

JT nodded. Nick hinted, but JT wasn't ready for that one-on-one.

After a bout of silence, Nick put down his weight. "Why don't you shower up? You've worked yourself enough for one day, don't you think?"

JT had to agree with him. He'd been worked over all right. The kiss flashed back in his mind and he tried to brush it away. "Yep. A nice cold shower sounds perfect."

****

JT rounded the corner of the Inn to find Norman hovering behind a bush. The little guy almost jumped a mile when JT called his name.

"Good Lord, man, you scared me to death."

JT stood next to him. "What are you doing hiding in the bushes anyway?"

A red glow reached Norman's cheeks. "Nothing." He started kicking the snow underneath his unusually small foot.

JT stretched around in the direction of Norman's interest. Missy stood on the porch sweeping. What do you know? Mary was right. "So you like her, do ya?"

Norman crossed his arms firmly. "No. I mean…well of course I like her. We work together."

JT couldn't help but enjoy Norman's misery. "I mean you like her—*like* her." His brows bounced up and down.

Norman's eyes fell to ground. "It doesn't matter. She's so beautiful, she could have her pick of any el-guy in the village. Why would she want me?"

JT swallowed back a laugh. "You'll never know if you don't ask her out."

Norman's head jerked up. "Ask her out?" His eyes bulged. "Are you crazy?" He shook his head. "No way."

"Yes way." JT grinned. "You gotta ask her out." JT stuck his hands in his pockets. "If I remember correctly, it seems I saw on the schedule there's a Christmas dance coming up."

Norman's face brightened. "Yeah. It's the biggest dance of the year." The corners of his mouth flattened. "But she'd never go with me."

"You never know if you don't ask."

They started walking toward the steps. As they got closer, JT whispered over his shoulder. "Here's your chance."

Norman elbowed him in the thigh. He'd probably shot for JT's side, but couldn't reach higher.

Missy looked up as they stepped on the porch. A smile brightened her face.

"Hello, Norman." Her cheeks turned pink.

She liked him, too.

"Hello, Missy. How's the…the…weather?"

JT sighed inwardly. *Epic fail.* He decided to help out the little dude. "Hello, Missy. I wondered if you were going to be singing at the dance. My wife and I think you sing terrific."

She blushed again. "Thank you, Mr. Walker. It's very kind of you to say."

JT gave Norman a small shove, and mouthed *ask her*.

"Okay. See you, Missy." Norman rushed in the door, tripping over the threshold in his hurry.

JT followed. "What was that?"

Norman glared at JT. "Excuse me if I don't take romantic advice from a guy who's here trying to save his marriage."

"Ouch." JT shrugged. "I guess I deserved that." He

tilted his chin. "But it's obvious she likes you."

Norman's face lit up. "You think?"

"Yep."

Norman went to the window and watched Missy through the thin curtain.

"But dude, if you're not going to ask her out, stop with the stalking thing. It's a little creepy."

Norman glared at JT and moved away from the window. "Whatever."

****

Mary hit almost every store on Main Street. Adding a shopping bag with each one. She picked out a souvenir for her mom. A bracelet she just couldn't live without. She even bought a box of fudge for David. She totally ignored the blue button down shirt that would look great with JT's eyes. Nope. He didn't deserve a gift.

Coal is what he deserves.

The shopping excursion gave her what she needed, a cooling off period. She was pretty sure she'd shopped out JT's mean quitter speech and his stupid kiss. That hot, passionate, stupid kiss. Her lips tingled just thinking about it. Surely the most passionate kiss ever to brush against her mouth. *Stop thinking about it.* She had David.

David. David. David.

Maybe if she repeated his name enough he would stick in her brain and she could stop thinking about her husband. *Good grief. Ex-husband.*

She abruptly came to a halt on the sidewalk and pressed her eyes closed. Deliberately bringing David's face into her mind. This would be easy enough. She'd think about David kissing her instead of JT. David's

Christmas at the Rekindle Inn

face came to view. *There. That's better*. She pictured him kissing her. He kissed like he was licking his way to the center of a tootsie pop. Way too much tongue movement going on. *Yuck*.

Then JT's face overtook her mind's eye. He stood over her. His dark blue gaze roamed across her mouth. His lips closed in on hers. Her eyes flew open. *No. No. No.*

Geesh. Bad idea. Total backfire. Mary marched down the sidewalk again.

What if JT's kiss was the last good kiss she'd ever have? In her life? Her knees wobbled beneath her. She braced herself against a storefront window for balance. Her thoughts about JT were silly. Maybe after she got to know David better she could teach him how to kiss.

Yeah, right. Not with his ego.

Mary slowly banged her forehead against the glass window, wallowing in her future kissing misfortune. At least until the cute little ruby dress in the window of *Peppermint Chi*c diverted her attention. She leaned back for a better assessment. What an absolutely adorable creation. She frowned. Unfortunately it was red. JT's favorite color. Too bad. She loved it. She sighed pathetically. Then turned away from the window to walk back to the Inn. Every step Mary took was weighted, as if someone had a hold of her arm, dragging her backward.

What in the world? Mary stretched her leg to take a step but didn't get anywhere. She swung her head around to see if anyone had witnessed this weird phenomenon, but the streets were empty. She stood there frozen in place. She sucked in a deep breath and tried again.

She lifted her foot to take a step, but it wouldn't move. She was being pulled back toward the store.

"Could this place get any weirder?" she shouted to the sky. Mary surrendered to the magnetic tug and turned back the other way. Now she could walk fine. Mary slung open the glass door to the dress shop and went in. Bells jingled on the door behind her.

Clearly her subconscious played a trick on her. Telling her not to miss out on a beautiful dress because of its color. She liked red, too.

"Hello, Mrs. Walker." An older woman called out from behind the counter as if she'd been expecting her. Tall and thin, she wore huge studded glasses over her narrow beak-like nose. Her gray hair was pulled tight in a bun, and her lips looked permanently puckered. Mary didn't recall meeting her before.

"Hello." She managed a smile.

"I have a dress in the window that would look lovely on you," the woman said with a raised brow.

Wow. Mary's eyes darted from side to side. The wacky weirdness continued. Clearly she must have seen her admiring the dress just now.

The tall birdlike woman made her way from behind the counter and came to a stop in front of Mary. The clerk shifted her weight to her right leg and crossed her thin arms over her chest. She roamed one large eye along Mary's torso. "And I think it will be the perfect fit." Her tone sounded like a stern Catholic school teacher's.

"Great." Mary stood there feeling a hundred shades of awkward.

"Let me get it for you," she said with a practiced smile. She went to the window display to peel the dress from the mannequin.

The clerk returned with dress in hand. "It's quite a lovely dress. One of my favorites."

Mary glanced around the small store. "Where's your dressing room?"

The clerk muffled a laugh under her breath. "Oh my dear, there's no need to try it on. The dress was made for you."

Mary exhaled. Obviously this woman didn't know who she was dealing with. Mary never fell to pressured sales tactics.

"I'd still like to try it on before I buy it."

Mary may as well have been talking to the garland covered walls, because the woman took the dress to the register and began to ring it up.

"Don't bother. I think I've changed my mind." Mary plastered her best fake smile and turned to leave. Then she experienced that freaking invisible pull on her arm again. Her eyes locked with the pushy saleswoman.

The corners of the clerk's mouth slowly lifted. "I assure you, it will be stunning on you." Her words were unhurried and confident.

Mary plopped her hands on her hips and took two long strides toward the counter. "I appreciate your confidence, but I would like to see for myself, if you don't mind?"

The woman folded the dress and placed it in a white box filled with tissue paper, totally ignoring Mary. "Mrs. Walker. The day you put on this dress, your life will be filled with happiness." She closed the box and tied a silky red ribbon around it. She raised her brow. "I'm pretty sure, this *isn't* that day."

Good Lord, is anyone in this town normal?

****

By the time Mary reached the inn, she'd practically talked herself out of leaving Jollyville. Even though the crazies around the place should have had her running to the airport yesterday. Her lips pressed together. Maybe Mrs. Klaus' silly three key round-up had a purpose, after all.

Mary reached for the door of the inn when she caught sight of JT using a rocker at one end of the porch.

Norman came rushing out to her. "Let me get those bags for you, Mrs. Walker."

"Thank you," she said handing off her loot.

"I'll have these sent to your room," he said, then disappeared inside.

Mary slid her hands in her back pockets and slowly walked toward JT. She came to rest against the railing. JT stared blankly in the afternoon sky.

"Hey."

"Hey." His hands tightened around the ends of the rocker arms. Their gazes locked briefly before she looked away. "Mary. I owe you an apology for the cabin. I was harsh and I'm sorry."

What about an apology for the lip lock? Moments of silence past. *Apparently not.*

Her stare fell on his and his mouth twisted. "I guess this place makes me a little crazy."

"I know the feeling."

He chuckled. "For instance, I just wondered if I came out here at night, if I could catch a glimpse of a sleigh fly-over."

She smiled.

"And I bet if I looked closely enough I'd see the

glow of Rudolph's nose."

"Okay. Now you're just talking crazy." Her smile widened.

"More like this place gives me delusions." He stood and walked to her. He leaned against the railing beside her. His closeness caused her heart to ache. Spending close time with him hurt, for the past and for their impossible future.

"Think about it. Other than Mr. and Mrs. K, and a few carolers here and there, the average height of citizens of Jollyville is four feet two inches. I find myself on my best behavior when Mr. K is around." He reached over and wrapped Mary's scarf closely around her neck as if they were still together and he had a duty to protect her. They exchanged a glance that spoke volumes. She turned away. Doing her best to ignore the familiar emotion.

JT's hands latched on the rail. "I'm pretty sure my new buddy here is an elf, and somehow I'm okay with that." He brushed a broad shoulder against her. "But most importantly"—his eyes darkened a deeper shade of blue—"I keep forgetting the reasons that brought us here in the first place." He crossed his arms over his chest. "I keep forgetting a month from now, I'll be nothing to you but a memory."

Way to make me feel like crap. He didn't play fair. Dropping the divorce on her shoulders. He was part of the decision, too.

"I told you I hoped we'd leave here friends. And I crossed the friendship line and blew it. And I'm sorry." His voice lowered. "I know you're leaving. I saw your suitcases." He exhaled a loud breath. "Mary. I...I..." His mouth curved. "I'll miss you."

Clearly not what he started out to say. She knew it. She wiggled away from him. "To be honest I'm feeling a little insane here, too." She grabbed the railing. "I guess I have two choices. I can leave. Or I can stay."

Mary didn't miss the hope shooting across his face. *Why?* Why did her friendship mean so much to him?

She nibbled on her bottom lip. "If I do stay, I think maybe we need to spend a little less time together. It's making my head all jumbled up. And I really can't handle it." She pulled a smile from her basket of reality. "Let's face it, in five days we'll be back in Virginia. Back to our old lives."

She turned to face his warm gaze she'd sensed lingering on her. "You'll be back at your job, and I'll be back—"

"With David." His jaw clenched.

"Yes. With David." If she must use her relationship with David as a shield for her heart, then she would.

"How could you?"

His stare sent a chill down her already frozen spine. "How could I what?"

"How could you get involved with someone so fast? I mean, my side of the bed was still warm."

Anger raged through her. How dare he. She leaned into him and jabbed a finger in his chest. "You want the truth?"

"Hell yeah, I want the truth."

"Because…because…" Her anger dissipated. Only sadness remained. "Because, JT. When I'm with David, I forget how much I miss you." She didn't wait for a response. She turned and rushed to the doors. She stopped suddenly and turned back to him. She closed the distance between them in two long strides. "This is so none of your darn business, but I'm going to tell you anyway. David has never been in *our* bed. In fact, we haven't even gotten to that level in our relationship." Why did she give him the satisfaction of knowing such a thing? She wasn't sure, but somehow she needed him to know.

JT looked shocked and relieved. *Stupid man.* Did he not know her at all?

Mary turned away and ran for the door. She would not let him see her cry. She didn't stop running until she got to her room, closed, and latched the door.

Mary fell across her bed. Sobs racked her body. Cleary this was the reason Mrs. Klaus insisted personal problems stay off limits. At least her uncertainty over leaving or staying had been answered for good.

She needed her key. She needed out of this place. Mrs. Klaus' ideas were ridiculous. Ignoring the core problems only put blinders on the real issues.

A knock sounded at her door. "Mary, let's talk about this."

"Go away."

"Nope. Not until you talk to me."

"The only thing I need to talk to you about is getting your key."

"Mary, open up," JT's voice demanded.

"No."

Things were quiet for a moment, then she heard the sound of muffled voices. Then another knock at her door. This time softer.

"JT, please go away. I beg you."

"It's not JT, dear, it's me. Mrs. Klaus."

Great, just the person she needed to see. Mary crawled off the bed and opened the door. She glanced over the woman's shoulder for a sight of JT.

"I sent him downstairs for a cup of cocoa."

Yeah. Cocoa. There's a cure all for their problems.

Mary waved Mrs. Klaus in and then pulled her suitcase from the closet. Somehow while she'd been out, it had been unpacked and returned. "I'm sorry, but I need to go home."

"I understand."

Mary jerked around to see if Joy was being condescending. But her eyes held compassion as she stood firmly against the door. Mary put the suitcase on the bed, went to the drawers, and started retrieving her things. Surprisingly, Joy Klaus joined her. Helping.

Mary knew she owed her an explanation. "It's hard to be this vulnerable after you've been hurt so deeply."

Mrs. Klaus placed a stack of sweaters next to the suitcase. "Of course it is, dear."

Mary's eyes blurred with tears. "Mrs. Klaus, I'm sorry to disappoint you, but I can't do this." She swiped her cheeks. "I can't pretend months and months of hurt can be forgotten with a peppermint stick and a sleigh ride. You don't know what I've been through."

Joy straightened and pointed to a chair. "May I?"

Mary nodded. "Of course," she said and took her own seat on the edge of the bed.

"I think I may know what you're feeling."

Doubt it. But go ahead, give it a shot.

"You came here reluctantly. For your mother mostly and to prove to JT you wouldn't bow down to his challenge." She shook a pointed finger. "Not to mention, you left a very angry boyfriend behind."

"How did you…"

"As I said before, dear, we have our ways." Mrs.

Klaus crossed her legs and rocked her foot. "You hoped you would come here and find some much needed closure. With the way you and JT split up, you never had any."

Mary locked gazes with Mrs. Klaus' hazel eyes.

"Let me go even a little farther back in time." Her eyes warmed. She crossed her hands gently in her lap. "You worked so hard planning the surprise anniversary trip."

How did she know?

"You thought if you could get JT away from town, away from his job, he would be reminded how important you were to him, and he'd stop putting his career ahead of your happiness.

Anger raced through her. "Did my mother tell you this?"

"No. Your mother would never betray your trust." She went on. "You were so excited. The only thing standing between you and the paradise vacation was a simple drive-by to his jobsite. He promised he would meet you at the airport. He'd only be a few minutes."

How did she know these things?

"But the minutes turned into an hour and then another. Next thing you knew, you were flying to a dream vacation built for two, alone."

Mary stood. She paced the room. The hurt of reliving the horrible day was too much. "I'm not even going to try and rationalize how you know all of this." Her arm waved with stifled emotion. "Part of this magical place, I guess. But the truth is, I've never experienced pain as deep as I did that day," she cried. "I can't do it again, Mrs. Klaus. I can't pretend that the scars are gone."

"I don't expect you to, my dear."

"So you won't be upset if I leave."

"Of course I'll be upset. You see, sometimes I can see into the future, and the future I see for you two is a once in a lifetime."

"You need to look again. Maybe you are seeing me with David. Or JT with Whitney. But the two of us are done." Mary folded her arms around her chest. "JT and I, we have no future."

"Then, at least take this time to close your past."

Mary was confused.

"You can't very well move on with your life, your future, if you've never allowed yourself to deal with your past." She stood and walked to Mary, placing a soft hand on her arm. "You told JT to move out before you came home from the trip, and he obliged. Not once did the two of you sit down and talk about what happened. How you were feeling."

She sighed. "Please, Mary. If you get nothing out of this trip but closure, so be it. But don't go into your future dragging the baggage of your past along with it."

****

JT stood in the middle of the park feeling lost. Mary planned to walk out on him again. He side-kicked a snowman, sending clumps of snow everywhere. He was tired of taking two steps forward and five back. He tossed his head back. He surrendered. Time to toss in the white flag.

"JT. What's up, dude?"

JT closed his eyes and frowned at Norman's new slang. *Great. I've corrupted an elf.*

"Not much." *My life sucks. Again.*

"You just murdered Frosty." He raised a brow in

the demolished snowman's direction. "I'd say something's up."

JT looked at the scattered guts of the snowman and for a brief second wondered if he really did kill Frosty. "Sorry about that."

"How about you and I slip over for a nice cold beer?"

JT's head jerked around. "A beer? Like a real beer?"

Norman nodded.

"You're not tricking me with a glass of root beer or something are you?"

He shook his head. "Nope. I'm talking about getting a beer at the Snow Globe Bar and Grille."

"Did you say bar? A bar in Jollyville?"

Norman rolled his eyes and nodded again.

"Then what are we waiting for, buddy?" JT slapped his hand on Norman's shoulder. "Let me buy you a cold one."

Five minutes later, they were walking through the doors of the Snow Globe. A grin spread across JT's face as he stood there looking around. Not your typical bar. But it sold beer. That's all that really mattered. He followed Norman to a booth and slid in. A lumberjack-looking man walked over holding two mugs filled with green liquid. He set the mugs on the table. "How you doing tonight, Mr. Walker?" He shoved a hand in JT's direction. "Marley Scrooge. Nice to meet you."

JT shook Marley's hand. Besides his name, he seemed normal. He wore jeans and a green flannel shirt. He was much taller than Norman, and JT could see his ears. No points.

JT looked at Norman. But he just shrugged.

"Call me JT."

"Okay. JT it is. Well, if y'all need anything else, I'll be behind the bar." He smiled then walked away.

"Marley Scrooge?" JT asked Norman.

"Yeah. What's wrong with that?"

If he didn't know, JT sure couldn't explain it. Only in *tinsel town.* He picked up his mug and tapped Norman's glass. "Cheers." *Let the green beer flow.*

****

Mary lay four blinks from sleep when a commotion outside her bedroom sent her shooting up in bed. She tiptoed to her door to peek. JT leaned against the suite's main door. The only light in the room came from the fireplace. She watched his body wobble from side to side. *What in the world?*

"Mary, are you here?" His words were slurred. "Of course you're not. You left me, like you always do."

Was he drunk? Good lord, where did he find a place to get drunk in the North Pole? JT hardly ever got drunk-drunk. She watched in silence. He took a step in the room and tripped on the corner of the coffee table.

Yep. Drunk.

"Ouch." He grabbed his knee.

Mary covered her mouth to keep from laughing. Served him right. Big creep. He collapsed on the sofa. Half on, half off. Against all her better judgment, she went to help.

When she rounded the sofa, she could see his eyes were closed. Her hands fisted at her waist. *Unbelievable.* Passed out cold.

Mary picked up one large leg at a time and heaved them over onto the cushion. She untied his boots and used all her strength to tug them off.

She tossed them on the floor beside the sofa. She straightened and looked at the plastered man in drunken slumber. Even with his hair tousled and his mouth gaped open like a monkey, he looked handsome. His dark lashes shadowed his strong cheek bones. His nose sat straight over his full curved lips. The same lips that had kissed her into delirium earlier in the day.

She pulled the folded quilt from the back of the couch and covered as much of his huge body as she could. She sat on the edge of the coffee table and watched him sleep.

She knew Joy Klaus was right. She held too much hurt in her heart to be over JT. And the hurt ate her alive. She needed to find a way to come to terms with her feelings for Joseph Tanner Walker before she could move on with her life.

Mary took her fingers and gently brushed JT's hair away from his eyes. He grabbed her hand, and his eyes flew open.

Oh crap.

"Mary. My angel." He half smiled before his heavy lids closed again. The memory of his pet name for her, stabbed like a knife to her heart. It'd been a while since he'd call her Angel. More like the Devil, these days.

He brought her hand to his lips and kissed it. "I'm sorry I screwed everything up."

She pulled her hand away and stood, taking a step back.

"I love you, Mary." He slurred before nodding off in slumber.

Sure you do. That's why we're getting divorced.

Chapter 8

Mary answered the door early the next morning. Norman entered pushing the coffee tray. His normal cheerful self.

"Good morning, Mrs. W." He gave Mary a big grin.

"Good morning, Norman."

"Good to see you this morning." Norman's smile faded.

Had compassion flashed in his eyes? *Great.* Did everyone in town know she wanted to bail yesterday? JT's door opened. He strolled into the room looking pretty good for a guy who'd stumbled in a few hours before. Mary didn't know what time he'd gotten up and gone to his room. But the quilt had been folded and put back in place.

"Good morning." JT's tone was soft.

She smirked. Maybe his head did hurt just a little. She didn't know if she should be happy about that or feel sorry for him. "How you feeling this morning?" she asked as loud as she could without screaming.

Okay. Happy, it was.

His forehead wrinkled. "Okay, considering the amount of green beer Norman talked me into consuming last night."

Mary rolled her eyes. "No way are you going to blame sweet little Norman for you partying too hard."

"For a giant, your alcohol resistance is awfully low," Norman stated as he made his way to the door.

JT frowned. "Well, for a little dude, your alcohol tolerance is scary."

Mary bit back a chuckle.

"It's the peppermint stick," Norman said, swinging the door open. He had their full attention. Norman raised a brow. "Gross maybe, but it's the magic behind our green beer. No hangover."

Norman pointed to the coffee tray. "Mrs. K took pity on you and sent some headache medicine. Take the medicine, dude. You'll be glad you did." He bowed then left them alone.

"Did he really keep a peppermint stick in his beer?"

"Yep. All night." JT's eyes narrowed. "I told him it was gross." He rubbed his forehead with his thumb and forefinger. "Maybe I should have listened to the little sh—Norman."

JT wasted no time. He hurried over and uncapped the bottle of aspirin and dropped two pills in his mouth. He tipped his head and swallowed. He gulped them down without a chaser.

He poured the coffee. "Sorry I bailed on you last night," he said without looking up. "To be honest, I was pretty sure you wouldn't be here this morning when I woke up."

"You had the third key, remember?"

He winced again. "Sorry."

May as well leave her options open. He didn't need to know she'd decided to stay after the talk she'd had with Mrs. Klaus on closure.

Hopefully, Santa's wife knew what she was talking

about. Heck. They did have a ninety-nine point nine percent success rate.

"Actually. I've decided to stay a couple more days." She folded her arms. "You know. Sort out my past, so I can move on with my future."

JT's gaze flew to hers. He opened his mouth to speak, but evidently changed his mind.

Mary nibbled on her lip. Hating herself for wanting to know what he'd held back. The words didn't really matter. She glared at her husband, but he didn't notice. He'd gone back to his chore of pouring coffee.

Please let me have the strength to put you in the past.

****

JT wasn't sure what the magic pills Mrs. K sent to him held, but when the potion hit his blood stream, all signs of his green beer hangover disappeared. *Good.* He'd messed things up yesterday with Mary. He needed to be on his game today. No screwing up. She had one foot out the door already.

Cheer.

Cheer, was the magical word of the day. And evidently cheer had something to do with ice-skating, because that's where they were headed. Mary didn't speak as they walked to the pond. She hadn't said two words at breakfast either.

Break the ice. Say something clever.

Nope. He had nothing.

"Good morning, folks." Nick rushed alongside them, his smile bigger than normal. If that were possible. "It's the most wonderful time of the year, don't you agree?"

Mary smiled. "Yes. I suppose it is."

An invisible fist sucker punched JT in the gut. Mary was missing out on her favorite time of year, and she had him to thank for it. If the circumstances were different, she'd be eating up this tinsel town.

Make it up to her. It's not too late. The words rang in his head as if Nick had said them out loud. But he hadn't.

JT rubbed his thumb over his chin. *How do I do that?*

No answer came.

Nick winked as he hurried along past. "Have a holly, jolly day, you two."

"You seem to be in an awful hurry," Mary shouted to his back.

He glanced over his shoulder. "It's a busy time of year for me, my dear. Ho, ho, ho." He waved then disappeared into an alley.

"This is the strangest place I've ever seen." Her eyes sparkled as she turned to look up at JT.

And in that second, it all became crystal clear. He needed to stop thinking. Stop thinking about the future *and* the past. He needed to make sure Mary had fun right now. Right now at this very minute in Crazy-Christmas-Town. A devilish smirk crossed his lips.

Yep. I got it. Thanks, Nick.

****

The next few hours passed smoothly. Mary managed to avoid JT and all cleverly hung mistletoe. They occupied the same pond, but she ignored him. Instead, she focused on ice-skating. Moving her legs back and forth. Gliding her skates in perfect figure eights. She blocked out everything but the sound of the blades as they ripped grooves in the ice. No future. No past. Just right now.

The more she moved over the ice, the more comfortable she became. The three years of skating lessons in high school had paid off.

Thank you, Mrs. Klaus, for convincing me to stay.

It would have been a shame to miss out on such a lovely place. And plenty remained to be seen.

Mary contemplated a jump. Good heavens, it'd been years. But today she was feeling brave. She pressed into the ice with every push getting stronger. Faster. Faster. The wind whipped around her face causing her eyes to blur.

Now.

Mary lifted her body and flew into the air, looping around before landing on the ice on a shaky, but steady skate.

Yes! I didn't kill myself.

She laughed. She couldn't help it. Mary hadn't been this free in such a long time. She turned to the sound of applause. JT leaned against the railing, clapping. Cheering for her. His face lit in a brilliant smile.

"*Cheer* day," Mary whispered. Her fingers flew to her lips. Her body tingled all over. Like she'd been shocked by an electric eel. The quirky tingling feeling rushed down her spine. She found herself mirroring his smile.

A commotion arose from the opposite side of the pond, diverting Mary's attention. Norman, Missy, and a few other little people had made their way onto the ice. The girls wore red and the boys, green. Four of the guys were pushing goal posts into place on each end of the ice. Her smile widened. Oh yeah. This could get interesting.

When she skated over to the crowd Norman tossed her a red jersey and handed her a hockey stick. JT slipped a green jersey over his head.

"Girls against boys," Norman shouted. "You know the rules."

Well maybe *they* knew the rules, but she didn't. "Wait a minute. I'm all for girl power and everything, but is this fair?"

A basket of giggles came from the girls. "Don't worry, Mrs. W. We have a secret weapon." Missy pointed and Mary followed her finger. Mrs. Klaus skated to them wearing her own red jersey. She was covered in pads and a helmet. Her red and green plaid skirt flew in the wind. Mrs. Klaus tried to look ferocious, but she pulled off adorable instead.

"You girls ready to kick some booty?" Mrs. Klaus said swinging her stick back and forth.

Mary belly-laughed. Yep. This would surely be hilarious.

The next forty-five minutes of her life consisted of laughing, hollering, pushing and fighting JT for the puck. She couldn't remember the last time she'd had so much fun. Mrs. K was quite the secret weapon. Nothing got past *the puck slayer*.

"Final score, three to two," Missy yelled, earning a round of cheers from the girls.

"Thanks to Missy sliding the puck right between Norman's skates," a voice shouted.

All eyes turned to the small guy. Norman popped his hockey stick on the ice. "Oh well. If I have to get scored on, I'm glad it's to the prettiest girl I know." Poor Norman's face matched Missy's jersey.

Mary looked to JT. He winked.

"Shucks, Norman. You're awful sweet." Missy blushed and punched him in the arm.

Yes. A girl after Mary's own heart.

"Okay, my sweeties. I've got to get back now." Mrs. Klaus slapped her team with high-fives, and the boys, too. Then she skated off the ice, leaving Mary smiling behind her.

"What a lady," JT said over her shoulder.

She turned to him. His large body slid up next to hers. "I'd say she is." Her gaze moved back to Mrs. Klaus. "Full of surprises."

They glided to a nearby bench to remove their skates.

JT slapped her on the shoulder. "Congratulations, champ." His blue eyes danced with mischief. "How's about I buy you lunch to show you what a good loser I am?"

"Sure. Why not?"

****

Mary sat on the porch later in the evening, listening to her rocker beat across the boards, in a slow, soothing rhythm. She liked *Cheer* day much more than *Memory* day, for sure. JT had been much different today. He hadn't been pushy. Or cocky. He didn't call her a quitter. The best part was, he didn't throw David up in her face.

Nope. He'd been nice.

Her fingers traced the outline of her lips recalling the kiss from the cottage. Not once did he try to hold her hand, wrap his arm around her, or…try to kiss her. Uneasiness stirred in her belly. Mary jerked up straight. *It was* not *disappointment tiptoeing around her mind.*

She could *not* be disappointed JT hadn't tried kissing her.

Could she?

Talk about crazy.

Good heavens. How could JT know what she wanted when clearly she didn't have a clue herself?

A young couple came up the steps of the inn and they exchanged greetings with Mary. Probably going to the restaurant. It seemed to be a town favorite.

"Here you are," JT said, walking toward her. He made himself comfortable in the rocker next to hers. He held two small boxes. One she recognized. One she didn't. He handed her the one she'd never seen before. "Mrs. Klaus said we need to bring these to the tree lighting ceremony."

The ornaments from *Memory* day. *Wow.* She hadn't really given it much thought, but it never dawned on her they'd be exchanging. The blood raced to her cheeks. What if he thinks mine is stupid?

Oh well. Who cares?

****

JT stood with Mary, listening to Marley Scrooge, the mayor of Jollyville, give a little speech. "Looks like the entire town came out for this," he said glancing at the crowd. "Well, I'll be darned. This place has tall elves, too."

His comment earned him a light jab to the ribs and he laughed. Mary seemed happy again, and the fact made him glad.

"If you will assist me in the countdown, we will begin the illumination," Marley said, pointing to the twenty-foot tree.

"Four."

"Three."

"Two."

"One."

The countdown echoed throughout the park, followed by a unanimous *Aww* as the thousands of lights sparkled to life.

"It's absolutely beautiful," Mary said, leaning a warm shoulder into him.

"Yep." *You are*. He said looking down into his wife's beaming face. Her blue eyes held the reflection of the tree lights, and he couldn't remember a time Mary looked so *happy*.

"Mary. I don't want to make things weird, but I gotta say it."

Her expression froze.

"You look beautiful tonight."

Her lashes lowered, and a blush caressed her cheeks. "Thanks."

"Christmas looks good on you."

She turned big blue eyes up at him, and the bright smile returned. "This place is amazing"

JT nodded. He pulled a note out of his jacket. "Mrs. K wanted us to read this after the tree lighting." He unfolded the paper and held it toward the light. "It says we're supposed to open our gifts and place them on the tree." He raised a brow. "Seems simple enough."

His *dumb-jerk* alarm began buzzing. Maybe giving Mary a reminder of a time he'd been a big fat liar wasn't the brightest idea he'd ever had.

Stupid.

Panic filled his lungs. He needed a plan. He could accidently knock the box out of her hand and stomp on it before she had a chance to look at the ornament. He looked down. The spot Mary had occupied stood empty. His eyes scanned the area.

Too late.

Mary had snuck off to a nearby bench. Balled up wrapping paper sat in her lap, and she held the little arm-cast ornament in the air. Staring at it. Obviously confused. JT took a seat beside her. He leaned forward and rested his elbows on his knees. "Nick told me to think back to a time when I realized I couldn't live without you." JT rubbed his hands together. "The time I busted my arm up and you took such good care of me— that's when I knew."

"Because I cooked and cleaned for you?"

He forced his eyes to look at her. "No. Because I totally screwed up, and you loved me anyway." He dropped his head in his hands. Clearly the ornament had been a bad choice.

"My Dad's always held on to every stupid thing I'd ever done, but not you." He leaned back and stared into his wife's eyes. "I messed up, and you loved me anyway."

The ends of her mouth curved. "Actually, it's very sweet."

JT searched her expression to see if she joked. Her compassionate gaze told him otherwise.

"Your turn."

JT pulled her ornament box out of his pocket and relaxed against the bench.

"Your wrapping job is much better than mine."

She grinned.

He tugged on the end of a thin white ribbon tied around the outside, and it fell away. The paper crackled beneath his fingers as he opened the box. He grabbed the string and lifted the ornament for a better look. What was it?

"The signs." JT's insides warmed about twenty degrees. "One of the best days of my life." He relaxed further and crossed his feet at the ankles. "God, I was so scared you were going to say no."

Her hand slapped his thigh. "Why?"

Wasn't it obvious? "You deserved so much better than me." Their gazes locked. "Still do."

JT's gut clenched in regret. Regret for always putting work first. "I'm sorry, Mary." He looked away. "I'm sorry I wasn't a better husband."

Mary's eyes grew wide. He'd shocked her.

Her slender fingers wrapped around his arm and she opened her mouth to say something, but she didn't get the chance.

"Hello, you two."

They turned to see Nick and Joy Klaus approaching arm in arm.

JT's lips curved. "Mrs. K, I almost didn't recognize you without your hockey stick swinging in my face."

They laughed.

"You gotta watch this one. She's full of surprises." Nick pulled his wife in for a squeeze.

"She was today." Mary stood and hugged them both. "She was definitely our secret weapon."

Mrs. Klaus' face lit in a bashful grin. "Oh, sometimes I just need to remind Norman who's boss." She set a gloved hand across Mary's arm. "Are you two ready to hang your ornaments on our tree?"

JT and Mary exchanged a shrug.

"I hoped we'd get to keep them." Mary looked down at her ornament.

Wow. Now she'd shocked JT.

"The memory of love is special. We must share it with everyone." Mrs. Klaus slipped a hand in the bend of Mary's arm and ushered her away.

Why'd she want to keep his goofy ornament? She wanted to put the past in the past. At least that's what she said. A grin slid across his lips. Or maybe…just maybe, his wife had been bluffing.

Chapter 9

Trust.

Yeah right. Mary tossed the card on the table.

"Come on. You ready?"

Good grief. JT would drive her to a straightjacket. As soon as he read they'd be snowmobiling he acted like a little kid on Christmas morning being told he had to wait to open gifts. "I'm coming. We still have twenty minutes before we need to meet Norman." She grabbed her scarf and gloves.

"He might be early," he said, holding the door open for her.

She bit back a laugh. He did look cute in his boisterous excitement.

****

They rounded the corner of the general store, where they'd been instructed to go, and Norman waited there—early.

JT shot Mary an *I told you so* smirk.

"Morning, folks," Norman called out as they approached three snowmobiles. "Dude." He fist bumped JT.

Holy Christmas tree. JT was ruining poor Norman.

"Mrs. Walker, will you be comfortable driving your own sled or would you rather ride along with Mr. Walker?"

She stared at the three metal beasts with skis

attached to the bottoms and for a second, almost chickened out.

The machines were huge. Her blood pumped a little faster as she tried to decide what to do. She looked up and saw a bratty grin stretched across JT's face, and she found her courage. "I'll take my own, thank you."

JT smirked. "Don't *trust* me?" He played on today's magical word.

"Nope." She trusted him about as far as she could throw him. "Think back to last night and the ornament you made for me. Enough said."

She referred to JT's dirt bike accident. He bent over as if she'd sucker punched him. "Oh, my wounded pride." He straightened up and grinned. "I'll have you know I would have nailed the stupid jump if a branch hadn't been lying across the trail."

"Oh. Now a branch lay across the trail. After all these years, I don't remember you mentioning that." She tried to keep a straight face. "I'll ride my own. Thank you very much." Honestly, she had the utmost confidence in JT's snowmobiling abilities. It was having to press up against him with her arms wrapped around him all day she didn't trust.

Norman gave them a fast lesson on how to drive a snowmobile. It didn't seem too complicated. A throttle handle, a brake handle. How hard could it be? But once she straddled the machine she wondered if she'd miscalculated. The idea of controlling the metal monster had her quite intimidated.

You can do this. And she did.

By the time Norman led them away from town and toward the snow-covered foothills, she had the hang of driving. She didn't know if the adrenaline high or the scenery had her pumped up with a double shot of happy. But she craved the adventure.

Wow. Could she actually be having fun? Her lips twisted. Maybe being this happy wasn't such a good idea. She did a mental check on her keep-JT-out wall to make sure she hadn't let hers down. *JT's sneaky. Keep your distance.* She hit the throttle on her bike and put a little distance between the two of them.

Evidently he hadn't noticed. He bellowed a loud howl from behind her. Something he did when he enjoyed doing something cool. Mary fought the smile she felt creeping across her mouth, but she couldn't stop it. He seemed to be having fun, too. Then her gut responded with, *See, stupid, you're letting him in.* What could she have done? Not come along? Mary liked adventure, too. No matter what her gut had to say about it.

They approached a large oak tree with a big red ribbon tied around its trunk. Norman waved them over.

"Okay, folks. This is the end of the road for me. You have your maps. Follow the red and green ribbons on the trees lining the woods and you'll be fine. There will be lunch prepared at one of our other cabins halfway along the trip. You'll see it marked on your map. I'll see you this afternoon."

Mary's confidence dropped about three levels as she watched Norman return in the direction they'd just come.

"You lead the way, Mary. I'll follow," JT shouted over the roar of the bikes.

"Me?" She pointed a finger at her middle section. She didn't believe her leading would be a good idea.

"Yes. I *trust* you." He grinned.

Mary rolled her eyes. *Smarty-pants.* She pulled the map from her pocket to get her bearings. Seemed they were going to make one big circle. Stopping for lunch at the bungalow. She'd make sure to pull any hanging mistletoe down and toss it in the fireplace, first thing. She stuffed the map back in her pocket.

Well. Here went nothing. She hit the gas, and they climbed a snow-covered hill. Mary had seen pictures of Vermont and its stunning beauty, but the view awed her. They crossed miles and miles of snow-covered magnificence by the time they reached the first resting point. Perfect timing. Mary's legs were aching for a break. She shut off the snowmobile, but her ears still rang from the nonstop roar of the motors.

She peeled her frozen body off the sled and stretched her legs. *Oh, yes.* Her muscles relaxed as she rubbed her hands over her sore rump. Her nose had been beaten to death by a blistering cold wind. Adrenaline pounded through her veins leaving her legs wobbly.

JT climbed off his bike. "Having fun?"

She didn't lie. "I'm having a blast."

He flashed her a full white-toothed, dimpled grin, and her frozen chest defrosted a bit. He walked toward the edge of the landing and looked over the side. "Mary, come check this out." He waved her over.

She traced his steps. Her eyes widened when she saw the valley's occupants. A corral of large animals with huge antlers on their heads. They were bigger than deer and didn't look like elk. Red leather collars with bells hung from around their necks.

"Well, we've found where they keep the reindeer." JT sidestepped and bumped an arm against Mary's.

She squinted her eyes for better focus. "Look." She pointed with a slender finger.

There standing among the beasts stood Nick Klaus. Of course. He tossed feed to the reindeer and they showed their gratitude with friendly nudges against his shoulders. He patted each one on the head and scratched behind their ears.

Tingling. Again. "JT, there's something about this place that makes me feel strange."

"Like little electric shocks all over your body."

Her eyes flew to his. "Yes. Just like that."

"Yeah. I've felt it, too. Right now even."

Thank goodness. At least she wasn't the only one losing her sanity. "Let's go. Watching Nick without his knowledge feels like an invasion of privacy."

"I was thinking the same thing."

"We don't want to interrupt Santa feeding his reindeer."

He chuckled. "Good God, we've totally lost it, haven't we?"

She nodded. "I'm having Mom committed when we get back."

"If we keep going on like this, our parents will have *us* committed."

They climbed back on the snowmobiles. Mary glanced at JT.

"Next stop, the toy factory."

She couldn't help but laugh.

According to the map, they were to follow the edge of the forest for about a half hour, then they should be at the bungalow for lunch. Good. Mary's stomach growled.

JT waved for her to lead again. Sure. She kind of

liked being in control for once.

Mary was too busy admiring the views to notice JT had fallen a little behind. When she glanced over her shoulder and realized he lagged, she let off the gas. The snowmobile didn't slow. How weird. She released her fingers from the throttle, but the machine still didn't slow. Her heart rate bumped up a notch. What was happening? She pumped the brake handle.

Nothing.

The snowmobile didn't slow at all. In fact it seemed to accelerate. Her shaking fingers clutched the handle bars in a death grip. She chanced a look over her shoulder, praying JT had noticed her dilemma. No. He seemed oblivious, staring at the mountains. Her pounding heart rattled her rib cage.

What do I do?

Come on, JT, look at me. Please. She mental telepathized him to look her way.

His gaze locked with hers. *Wow. It worked. Thank God.*

"Help!" she screamed as loud as she could, but the wind whipped the sound away. Her gaze darted to the front, but only for a second. She turned back to him. He must have recognized her panic. His legs were straight and he leaned forward on his machine, moving quickly up the mountain.

Relief soared through her, but she didn't understand why. What could he do? Once he pulled beside her, she screamed over the roar of the motors and her thumping heart. "Something's wrong." Her voice rattled with panic. "It won't slow down."

"Hit the brakes."

She wanted to scream, "I've tried that already,

genius." But her fingers squeezed the handle again anyway. Still nothing. She shook her head back and forth in disbelief. Nothing worked. Mary looked ahead. The snowmobile moved too fast. She needed to pay attention to her options.

She approached a long line of trees. *Don't cry. Crying won't help.* She braved a glance in his direction. He pointed frantically at something ahead. But his warning came too late. A low hanging branch hung directly in her path. The narrow rut gave her no wiggle room. She gripped her hands around the handlebars and held on for dear life. The limb swooped across her body almost knocking her off. A sharp pain ripped across her arm as the branch made contact.

Tears burned her eyes. *Jump off.* She'd have to jump off. But she couldn't. Her gaze flew to the bottom of her sled. The ground passed beneath her at record speed. She gripped the handlebars tighter.

Oh God. She'd die at the North Pole. The trees were close. She moved too fast to think.

JT's voice rang out over her hammering fear. She tried to hear him and keep the machine in control at the same time.

Their gazes locked.

"Jump. I'll grab you." His stern tone demanded she listen and respond. He held out his hand.

No way. They'd both be killed. She tore her gaze from his. The trees were no more than fifty yards away. If she attempted the turn to miss them, she'd fly off into the forest for sure.

Oh God. What do I do?

Her eyes zipped back and forth from JT to the forest. His sled runners almost touched hers.

Certain death moved closer.

Thirty yards.

Twenty yards.

She looked back at him. His jaw was clenched, his eyes narrowed.

"Take my hand." Frustration echoed with every word. "Do. It. Now."

Oh, God help us.

Before she could talk herself out of it, she latched onto his hand. He yanked hard, jerking her toward him. She flew across the sled, but her legs and feet dragged across the thick snow. His grasp was strong, but she couldn't hold on.

Alarm paled his expression. He hit the brakes to slow the bike with his other hand, but before he could bring it to a stop, Mary felt her fingers slipping. He tightened his hold, but to no avail. She slipped from his grasp and slid down the hill, body rolling to a halt, landing on her back. She stared up at the sky in disbelief. Her body ached all over, but she was alive.

JT stopped his machine, jumped off, and rushed to her side, falling on his knees beside her.

"Mary, are you okay?" His expression was shadowed with panic.

She was able to nod. He pulled her carefully into his arms. Resting her head against his chest.

Safe. Oh my God. She was safe.

She looked up just as her snowmobile crashed into the trees. The sound of crunching metal and cracking branches echoed across the mountain. The sled flew up in the air and tumbled over, settling upside down in a clump of branches. She squeezed her eyes shut and nestled her face further into his shoulder. The sound of her heartbeat pounded in her ears, and her body trembled all over.

His strong arms held her tight as sobs rattled her body.

He saved her. JT saved her life.

He stroked the back of her head. "It's okay, babe. It's okay." His voice shook, but the tone sounded strong. He held her until her crying subsided, reassuring her repeatedly that he wouldn't let her go. "God, you scared me. I thought I'd lost you."

Mary didn't know how much time passed before she could move. Breathe. Ease her death grip hold. She opened her eyes and tilted her head to find JT staring back at her.

"Are you sure you're not hurt?" His dark blue gaze wandered over her face. He ran his thumb slowly across her cheek. He cupped her chin for a better look, turning her head slightly one way then the other. She noted the fear in his eyes. He'd been frightened for her life, too.

Her insides warmed. There was something oddly captivating about almost being killed, then being rescued by your husband. "My arm hurts." She winced as fire pierced her right triceps.

"Can you stand?"

She nodded, and he helped her to her feet. She could stand fine, and the rest of her body felt okay, only her arm ached.

"Do you think you can you ride?"

She knew she could ride physically, but figured he worried more about her mental state.

She nodded. "Only if you drive really slow."

He leaned in to brush a soft kiss on her forehead. "You got it." The warmth of his breath lingered on her skin.

When his gaze settled on hers again, the fear she'd seen moments ago had been replaced with something else. His eyes reflected a familiar expression she hadn't seen in a long time. Concern? Compassion? Could it be love? *No. Of course not.* She lowered her eyes. The close call had her seeing things.

He loosened his grip. "Let's take a minute so I can get a look at the map and figure out where we are."

Mary nodded. The near death experience had driven them off-course. Her body still rattled with nerves as she found her footing. His stare landed on her torn jacket, then he glanced up to her face.

"It's fine. Just get us out of this cold."

He placed a strong hand against the small of her back and led her toward his snowmobile.

JT scanned the map, then the area. "The cottage should be about a mile around the bend." He pointed in that direction. "Maybe if we're lucky we can catch Norman preparing it for lunch. You ready?"

Heck no. She never wanted to see another snowmobile as long as she lived. Much less ride one. She'd walk the mile on foot if her body didn't shake uncontrollably.

"Babe. I promise, I will not let anything happen to you."

She searched his eyes for reassurance and knew he meant every word. She nodded.

He climbed on first, and Mary mounted behind him. She locked her arms around him clinging for dear life, suffering through the agonizing pain throbbing in her right arm.

He clasped her hands in his before he started the

sled. Then he took off at a slow pace. "Don't worry. I'll get us there safely."

Mary couldn't pull her gaze away from her demolished snowmobile as they drove past. Bile churned in her stomach, and she fought the sickness away. She closed her eyes and pressed her cheek into JT's strong back. *Please get us there soon.*

They reached the cabin a few minutes later.

"Thank you, God," Mary whispered and rushed to dismount as the snowmobile came to a halt.

JT wrapped a sturdy arm around her and guided her into the cabin. She welcomed the warmth his body offered. She refused to admit how much she enjoyed his devoted attention.

Heat greeted them at the door, warming Mary's frozen body. The tension in her sore muscles eased.

"Looks like we missed Norman." His jaw clenched. "Stand here a second." JT took two long strides toward the fireplace. He used a poker to stoke the fire into a blazing flame. Mary pulled off her gloves and unzipped her jacket. She wanted her stifling snow gear off, but her injured arm meant she needed assistance.

"Wait." He slipped out of his own jacket. "Let me help you." Once he tossed his things in a pile, he guided her to a chair. She plopped down, and he reached for her leg. He started loosening her boots. His hands worked slow and easy as he removed one. Then the other. He pointed to her snow pants. "Unsnap your pants."

Good grief. A blush reached Mary's cheeks as she popped the silver button. *You have stretchy pants underneath. Calm down.*

JT's gaze locked on her unbuttoned snap, and she experienced a different kind of panic. *Hold on.* She could undress herself. Having JT do it seemed weird. And dangerous. But when JT tucked his fingers in the waistband, she didn't stop him. He wiggled the pants down over her hips. She closed her eyes and fought against the familiar excitement that accompanied JT taking her clothes off.

Ignore it. Ignore it.

She nibbled on her bottom lip. The pants slid across her feet, and he tossed them aside.

She didn't have much time to feel guilty for enjoying the feel of JT's hands on her body because he reached for the jacket next. Excruciating pain yanked her mind back to reality.

A loud moan escaped her lips. He froze.

"Crap." JT's tone reverberated worry. "Let's get a plan. I think your arm may be pretty banged up."

You think?

"Let's do this together, slow and easy."

She nodded. First he pulled off the good sleeve. Then the torn one. He moved gently, but her arm throbbed from her shoulder to her elbow. She inhaled some deep breaths as he slid the jacket down her arm. She slammed her eyes shut and prayed for relief. Finally the jacket came off. He pitched the garment into the pile of discarded snow clothes. Mary's gaze darted to the cut on her arm. Blood edged her ripped shirt, but she couldn't see the wound.

He carefully pulled the shredded material to the side.

He grimaced. "Shit."

His gaze flew to Mary's.

"What?" His reaction freaked her out. "Is it bad?" She glanced toward the crimson sleeve. The wound radiated pain in full force. She could feel warm, sticky liquid dripping down her arm.

JT raced to the bathroom. The sound of banging cabinets followed. All the beating and banging sounded like he tore the place apart.

She collapsed against the chair, carefully propping her elbow on the armrest. Where were Santa and his sled when they needed him?

He rushed back in the room with a first aid kit under his arm and a bowl of water balanced in his hands. A washcloth had been slung over his wrist and his face sported one serious expression.

"I found a bottle of Mrs. K's magic aspirin. I think we should start with that." He took two pills from the bottle and handed them to her, followed by a cup of water.

Mary swallowed them, hoping for a fast reaction.

"Okay. Let's take off your shirt."

"What?" Her gaze flew to his.

He lifted a brow. "Don't get all shy now. It's not like I haven't seen what's underneath."

She blushed. Why couldn't they cut off the sleeve? Then oozy wet material touched her side. She'd bled through the side of her shirt, too. "Fine."

JT was as gentle with the shirt as he'd been with the jacket. The shirt fell free.

"You okay?"

No, she wasn't okay. She sat in a cozy bungalow with her soon-to be-ex wearing nothing but a red lacy bra and a pair of stretchy pants.

Mary nodded regardless. She watched as JT gently

wiped the blood away. The cut extended three inches or more around her arm, and an ugly purple bruise had begun coloring the area.

"It's long, but I don't think it's too deep." Concern echoed in his voice. "Maybe in the middle." He twisted his lips. "Probably could use a few stitches."

"I'm sure it's fine."

He looked through the first aid kit. "There are some butterfly bandages in here. Hopefully this quick fix will do until you can see a doctor."

She closed her eyes to the overwhelming pain, as JT put a glob of antibiotic ointment on the wound. He butterflied it the best he could, then wrapped a white gauze bandage around her arm. Every step came along with a few "Are you all right? Am I hurting you?" questions.

JT may be a butthead workaholic, but deep down he was a nice guy. Compassionate. Caring. She'd forgotten how sweet he could be when she wasn't feeling well.

A frown crossed Mary's lips. Funny how discontentedness had a way of replacing all good with only bad.

JT taped the end of the bandage, then leaned back on his knees. "You good?"

Mary nodded once more. For the first time since he'd become a bungalow EMT, he let his gaze roam over her. A blush warmed her cheeks as his gaze lingered on her lacy bra.

His eyes darkened, and his jaw clenched. She recognized the look from years of marriage. A passionate stare slowly worked its way up her person. Her body tingled with his every glance. Maybe it was the accident. Maybe the magic in the air. Mary wasn't sure, but she knew one thing. She wanted her JT back. She'd almost died on the mountain today. Now she chose to live.

She wanted to run wild fingers through JT's dark mane. Her gaze lowered to his chest. *Yep.* She wanted to explore every glorious inch of his body with her hands. Her mouth. Her breath quickened. Mary's chest heaved up and down with anticipation. Her gaze worked back to his full lips. God, she wanted to kiss those lips. Her eyes searched out his.

Tense dark blue orbs stared back at her.

What? Are you feeling it, too? Show me something.

His hand slipped behind her neck and pulled her to him. He tilted his head until she could feel his breath on her lips. He stopped with his mouth so close.

He awaited her approval. And she gave it to him. Mary slid her fingers behind his neck and pulled him closer. One last look before his lids closed, and his mouth found hers. His lips were warm and soft. He began gently, then passion took over, and his kiss became demanding. Pleading. Urgent.

She kissed him back, matching every ounce of desire he gave. Her hormones burned as his tongue worked its magic. He broke away from her. He reached for the thick blankets folded on the sofa and spread them across the rug in front of the fire. He picked her up and laid her gently on the blankets, taking his place beside her.

Mary's nerves had her fingers shaking when she reached out to caress JT's cheek. The unbridled desire to make love to her husband came as a surprise. Rekindling the love between them excited her and scared her to death simultaneously.

His warm mouth swept over her ear, then shifted to the downy skin of her neck. The tingling sensation grew, as his lips moved lower. His tongue brushed the roundness of her breast peeking from under her bra. He unsnapped the bra's clasp, carefully sliding the red straps down her arms before tossing it to the side.

Her pulse raced and her breath hitched as the realization of what was about to transpire between them came to full focus. She was opening herself up to him. Pulling her heart from her chest and handing it over. It was barely pieced together from being shattered from before. He was entering vulnerable ground she swore she'd never again allow him to go. But none of that seemed to matter now. The hurt, the anger, had vanished on that mountainside. She wanted to make love to her husband without the boundaries and walls of her own insecurities standing between them.

JT slid her pants down her long slender legs taking her panties along with them. He tossed the clothes aside. His hand wound back up her legs pausing at the apex of her thighs. Her body shuddered when his finger slid into her folds of soft flesh. Her pulse pounded in her neck, and her core throbbed with uncontrolled need. He'd touched her there a million times, so why did it feel like the first?

His dark blue gaze lingered on her naked breasts, his blatant stare electrifying her. Slowly his head descended, and his mouth hovered over the peak of her nipple. The warmth of his breath teased her until she couldn't take another second. Her hand slipped around his neck and pulled him down to her. She wanted to feel his mouth on her. Licking and sucking.

A moan skated from her lips as he appeased her with his mouth. She ran her fingers through his dark hair as his attention moved from one breast to the other, careful to keep her injured arm still.

His lips found hers once more as his fingers gently stroked her. She groaned against his mouth and her flesh ached, ready to trust him with her love. His kiss was warm and exhilarating. His tongue tangled with hers in a dance of passion. JT pulled away, ending the kiss. Her eyes flew open wondering why he'd stopped. His heated gaze lingered on hers, telegraphing his intent. He was giving her one last chance to change her mind.

"Please." The word escaped her lips in a dry whisper. His stare roamed her face, then settled on hers. One corner of his mouth turned up, and he pressed a gentle kiss against her forehead.

He rose to his feet taking the warmth of his body with him. Mary followed his every move as he efficiently stripped. Seeing his hard, muscled chest again, anticipating how it would feel pressed against her, made her swallow past a dry lump in her throat. Their gazes tangled as his hands fumbled with his zipper. As he stood there naked, she questioned how she'd taken the wonder of his body for granted. His rampant erection shot a surge of satisfaction through her veins. Her legs drifted apart, inviting him closer. He joined her on the pallet of blankets, covering her body with his own, supported by strong biceps.

JT slid inside her. The fullness of him made her gasp. She gripped his shoulders for balance from the overpowering twirl of emotions churning within her. The pain in her arm throbbed, forcing her to release her hold.

With each thrust, Mary's mind spun; her breath reduced to quick pants. As they moved together, she wondered if JT could see into the inner depths of her emotions. This colossal emotional link they were sharing was new and unexpected.

She closed her eyes to blink away unexpected tears. Oh God, she'd missed him. The months alone and this sense of having rediscovered something precious, combined with JT's loving touch overloaded her senses.

The rhythmic feel of his body moving along with hers in an intimate dance was more than making love. This time their act was passionate, almost magical. The beauty of it made her heart feel as if it would fly from her chest. That was the last conscious thought Mary had.

The sounds of moans and the quiet crackle of the wood fire filled the room. JT's pace quickened. His lips moved over hers. They exchanged kisses, their tongues tangling as his strong hand slipped under her hip bringing her body even closer to him.

She couldn't control her yearning or her reactions any longer. She arched her body against his as her release quaked throughout. JT experienced his own climax a moment later, and their bodies convulsed together. After, his arms shook, and he lay carefully on her, panting and covered with a light sheen of perspiration.

When JT's breath calmed, he rolled to his side taking Mary along with him, careful with her injured arm. She molded against him, settling her head on his shoulder. Her hand rested in the center of his chest, feeling the strong thump of his heartbeat beneath her fingertips. *What a day.* The sudden aching in her arm was a reminder that she'd almost lost her life. Yet, she was living for the first time. Mary wasn't sure what was in store for the two of them, but she knew she'd cherish this memory with JT for the rest of her life.

They didn't speak. There was no reason. Everything that needed to be said had just been spoken without words.

****

JT woke with Mary's naked body entwined with his. Had he been dreaming? If he had, his mind played a cruel trick. He nestled his face into her long blonde hair. Mary's soft locks brushed against his lips. Nope. No dream. He traced a gentle finger down her bare arm, skipping over the bandage. The bruise showed from underneath the wrapping.

The accident flashed back in his mind and the crushing panic filled his chest. He closed his eyes with the memory. He thought he'd lost her for good. He realized in those terrifying moments that Mary meant everything. More important than his job, his father.

Only Mary mattered in his life. He would win her back if it was the last thing he did. He dreaded her waking up. What if she'd only made love to him as a result of her almost dying? His heart raced. What if she decided she'd made a big mistake?

He saw her blink. Guess he'd find out.

She looked up at him. A blush crossed her face. There was a twinkle in her eyes.

"Hi."

Good sign. "Hey."

"What time is it?"

He waited for her to pull out of his arms. But she

didn't. So far, so good.

JT glanced at his watch. "Three o'clock." They'd been there two hours. Asleep for about half. She took a finger and ran it slowly down his chest, electrifying his every nerve along the way. He pressed his mouth against hers. Her lips were warm and soft. Their mouths parted, and his tongue entwined with hers. His groin responded to the wet, hot kiss. He thought he'd never feel her beneath his skin again. Never run his fingers through her long blonde hair. Kiss the soft flesh at the nape of her neck. JT's palm found the roundness of her breast and squeezed gently until she whimpered beneath his lips.

He lifted his head to take advantage of the firelight and let his gaze roam slowly over his wife's nude body. He'd missed her. Missed the slender curve of her waist. Missed the round tightness of her hips. The beautiful pink shade of her nipples. He caressed one between his forefinger and thumb, and Mary's breath quickened. His mouth took place of his hand, and he didn't stop there. He was determined to get reacquainted with every inch of soft flesh. He'd taken for granted just how passionate and sexy she was in the past, but never again.

Yes. *Trust* day was his favorite day, by far.

Later on, as he laid on his back holding her in his arms he heard her belly rumble. "Hungry?"

"Starving."

That was all he needed to hear. He'd worked up quite an appetite himself. He helped her dress, giving her the t-shirt he'd worn under his flannel. Then assisted her to the table.

They were just finished eating when they heard

ringing bells approaching. The jingle reverberated as if they were overhead. Their gazes flew to the ceiling but the noise faded away. A frantic pounding sounded at the door moments later.

When JT opened the door, Norman came flying in the room, Nick Klaus on his heels.

"Oh, thank goodness," Norman wailed after giving Mary and JT the once-over. "When you didn't come back, we began searching. We saw the snowmobile and—" Norman couldn't finish his sentence. He collapsed in a chair and rubbed a slow hand across his perspiring forehead.

Nick rushed toward them. "Are you kids okay?"

JT jumped in. "I'm fine, but Mary cut up her arm pretty good."

His statement had Norman on his feet again running to her side. Mary lifted her sleeve to show the bandage. A large circle of red seeped through.

"Oh no. That looks—" Norman didn't get the chance to finish that sentence either. His face turned white, and his eyes rolled back in his head. He went down for the count.

JT grabbed him before he hit the floor and carefully placed him on the sofa.

Nick chuckled. "He's a wimp when it comes to the sight of blood, I'm afraid." Nick turned back to Mary's arm. "We need to get you back to town and let Doc take a look at you."

Mary blushed. "Sorry about the snowmobile. The throttle got stuck and…"

Nick placed a gentle hand on her shoulder. "Please, my dear. I should be apologizing to you. When I think of what could have happened." He shook his head and frowned. Probably the first time since they'd been there that Nick wasn't…jolly.

Nicks words brought back the drama of the accident for JT. His knees wobbled. He slid into a chair. *Move over, Norman; evidently, I'm a wimp, too.* Mary walked over and placed a hand lightly across the nape of his neck.

"JT saved my life." She leaned in and kissed the top of his head. JT relished the warmth of her touch. He grabbed her hand and brought her around to sit on his lap. She didn't protest.

Nick's face lit up like the town's Christmas tree on illumination night. "I see."

He saw all right. He seemed as pleased as JT at the change of events. "Did I hear the sleigh outside?"

Nick nodded.

Her expression calmed. "Is there any way I can hitch a ride? The idea of getting back on a snowmobile is a little overwhelming at the moment."

Norman had come to, and a normal shade of elf pink returned to his cheeks. "Don't even think of it, Mrs. Walker. I'll drive the snowmobile back for you. You and Mr. Walker ride back with Sant—Mr. Klaus."

She smiled at JT and the knot in his chest rose again. The one that reminded him that as rapidly as she'd forgiven him, she could just as quickly go back to hating him. This sucked. He wanted to be happy, but his heart kept him on don't-break-me-again alert.

****

Mary sat on an examination table at the small emergency hospital in Jollyville as the doctor treated her arm. Funny, she'd never noticed the health center before. The serious little man they called Doc smeared globs of salve on her wound. White frizzy hair shot out from under an old-fashioned reflector mirror strapped to his head.

Doc had to stand on a stool to reach the examining table. "I'm pretty good, but I think this may leave a scar, regardless," he said, then set down his jar. He gently placed a gauze dressing over the cut then wrapped her arm with an ace bandage.

"No stitches?" Mary glanced down at her arm. She thought she'd need a couple.

Doc glared at her over his silver rimmed glasses. Clearly not liking her doubt in his judgment.

Mary was relieved. "Great. I hate getting stitches."

He frowned and jumped off his stool. "You should be fine in two days."

Two days? Mary didn't agree. Her injury hurt like heck.

"Now. I want you to rest for a couple of days. No more adventures for you for at least twenty-four hours. I'll send word to Mrs. K so she can adjust your schedule."

Her cheeks warmed. That awkward feeling of everyone in Jollyville knowing what took place at the Rekindle Inn crept along her spine. Mary slid off the examination table. "Thanks, Doc."

For the first time since she arrived at the hospital, the man's mood seem to relax. "Now don't lift a thing with your arm for a good while."

She nodded in understanding. Mary had a feeling she didn't have to worry about lifting anything. JT hovered around her like a low-flying cloud, since the accident. Doing everything for her before she had a chance to think. She half smiled. She didn't know how this crazy Christmas town and its silly list of rules had worked magic. But she was back with JT.

Wait. Were they back together? They'd had sex, but what did that mean really? *Crap.* Her heart sped up a notch. She didn't even know if they were *rekindled* or not. How had this happened?

"You feeling okay, Mrs. Walker? You look a little pale." Doc grabbed her arm to provide balance.

Mary leaned back against the table. "Yes. I think so." How could she ignore the last six months as if they hadn't happened? The last year for that matter?

"Doc. Maybe I need to be admitted. Clearly, I must've banged my head in the accident."

"What did you say?" Doc shot her a worried stare.

She patted the top of his hand. "Nothing." She managed a smile. "I'm fine."

Chapter 10

Healing.

Looked like Mrs. Klaus got the message. Mary set the card back on the coffee tray. She didn't get a chance to see Joy when they finally returned to the inn the night before.

She glanced in her room. JT's large body sprawled across her bed. Heat stirred her belly. Being with him for the past few hours had boggled her mind. They'd been together for days, but since the recent turn of events, a huge shift had occurred. Her thoughts whirled trying to determine what the change meant. The feeling was bigger than a reconciliation. More as if they'd been together for the very first time. Free from the reality of life.

Reality. Good grief.

What would happen when the trip ended and they returned to their real lives? Disaster, that's what. Mary's pulse pounded in her temples. Her breathing quickened. She was light-headed. She paced in front of the fireplace.

"Hey. Is everything okay?"

She turned to him. He rubbed sleepy eyes, standing before her in nothing but a pair of jeans. His bare chest drew her gaze. She'd always loved the way his stomach muscles trailed to a glorious vee disappearing into the waist of his pants. Her body craved a repeat of the enchanting night before.

Had her common sense been blinded by lust?

"Mary. You okay?"

No. Everything is upside down.

She needed to speak with Joy Klaus, and she needed to do it—now.

"I'm going to see if Mrs. Klaus can give me advice on what I should wear to the dance tomorrow night." *Crap.* She was lying to JT already. Maybe not. She could always ask about wardrobe when she talked to Mrs. K.

"Right now?" He took a step toward her.

"Yep. Right now." She went to the closet and pulled out her coat.

"You want me to come with you?"

Um. Heck no. She shook her head back and forth.

"Okay." He hurried over and helped her slip on her jacket. "Well, take it easy on the arm."

A quick shot of pain reminded her of how far she'd come, and how much she still needed to heal.

He pulled Mary in his arms. Oh, he felt good. For a second she considered throwing her doubt and concern down the chimney, and crawling back under the covers with him. But fooling around wouldn't help her with the state of *oh my God, what are we doing*? she had to resolve.

He leaned closer to kiss her. Mary's mind whirled with their shared passion.

Go now before you can't. She pushed free of his embrace. "I'll only be a little while."

He smiled down at her, and her belly flip-flopped. She was falling in love with JT, all over again. Her heart raced. Short, rapid gasps of air replaced her normal breathing. *Yep.* A panic attack was imminent.

No. No. No.

Mary needed air. She hurried to the door. When she turned to him, a fearful expression had settled over his face. He sensed her distress. *Oh, shoot.* She forced a smile. "I just need to...ah...go...see Mrs. Klaus for a minute." She waved her finger toward the door hoping he'd fall for her *everything's fine* cover up.

Yeah, right. She turned and left before he had a chance to put her excuse to the test.

Mary searched for Mrs. Klaus throughout the inn to no avail. She stood in the lobby contemplating her next move when Norman rounded the corner.

"Hello, Mrs. Walker." His spirits seemed brighter than normal. "How's the arm today?"

"It's fine. Norman, I'm looking for Mrs. Klaus. Do you know where I can find her?"

He diverted his eyes. "I'm sorry, but Mrs. K won't be in until this afternoon."

No. He had to be mistaken. She was *always* at the inn. A nervous whistle sounded from her little friend. Mary tried to make eye contact, but Norman looked in every direction but hers.

Norman was hiding something.

"Norman. I really need to see her. It's important."

"Sorry. There's been an emergency at the bakery. She'll be tied up all day."

"Mrs. Sugar Plum's bakery?" The shop stood right across the street.

Norman shook his head. "No."

"Then what bakery?"

Norman's face paled, and his little feet knocked together.

"Norman, what bakery?"

He rolled his eyes. "Mrs. Walker, I'd love to tell you, but I just can't. I've already said too much."

Mary squatted to his level. "Norman, I wouldn't ask you if it wasn't really, really important."

He scanned her face in contemplation. His gaze settled on her injured arm.

She couldn't believe she'd resort to manipulation, but a girl had to do what a girl had to do.

"I need to ask her about my arm." She reached up and rubbed her triceps.

"What about Doc? He's around."

"No. This is more of a woman-to-woman thing."

His little cheeks flamed red. "She's at the factory's bakery." His lashes lowered to the floor.

He'd given her more information than he should. His expression made it obvious. Guilt pinched her gut, but she ignored the remorse. She didn't have time to feel like a jerk. Right now, she desperately needed to talk to the matron of Crazy Christmas Town.

"Norman, can you take me there? I'm having a bit of my own emergency, and I really need to speak with her."

He frowned. "I'm sorry, Mrs. Walker, but the factory isn't open to the public."

Shoot. Shoot. Shoot. This couldn't happen. "I'm really not *the public*. Plus, if she's having an emergency, maybe I can give Mrs. K a hand?"

Norman tapped his small foot on the floor. She hoped he considered her request.

"Let me give Mrs. K a call. If she gives me the okay, I'll take you out there."

Great. Mary released a thankful breath. She

grinned as he pulled a candy-cane shaped cell phone from his pocket and dialed.

"Hello, Mrs. K. It's me, Norman. Mrs. Walker wanted me to bring her out there to you. She's like really, really needing to talk to you. She said it's important."

Mary waited, her nerves in knots. *Please. Please. Please.*

"Yes, ma'am." Norman hung up the phone. "You ready?" Norman's question left her stunned.

Would she actually get to see *the Toy Factory*? Of course not. There was no toy factory. Only a factory. A lot of towns had factories. Lord, she'd lost her mind along with her heart.

Mary and Norman headed to the biggest building in Jollyville. Mary had passed it a million times but never really looked at it. The gold plaque above the door read *The Factory*.

"Hmm. Very interesting."

"What?" Norman asked as they climbed the steps to the building.

"Oh, nothing." She smiled at her short companion.

Norman opened the door. Inside was a huge foyer with four doors. Two green, one red and one white. Mary reached for the door knob of the red one.

"No. No. No. Not that one." Norman threw his little body against the door. He braced himself firmly in the center, his fingers latched tightly to the frame.

Mary swallowed a giggle.

"That one." He nodded to the white one without releasing his steady grip.

"Thanks, Norman." Mary opened the white door and walked inside. The bakery looked like a huge version of an everyday kitchen. Nothing appeared odd but its size. Mrs. K sat at a table mixing a gigantic bowl of cookie batter.

"Hi, Mary. Come on in." Joy Klaus put her spoon down and wiped her hands on her candy-striped apron. Mary made her way into the room. Good gracious. The room was odd after all. Hundreds of cookies were everywhere. Some on cooling racks. Some as raw dough waiting for the oven. Most already packaged in little white boxes, tied with red ribbon.

"Wow. Looks like you've been busy." Mary resisted the urge to grab a warm cookie from the rack and plop it in her mouth.

"Our baker is out sick today. He supplies the daily cookies for the el—for our workers."

Mary was positive Mrs. K had begun to say elves, but that would make her new friend crazy. And Mrs. Klaus was too perfect to be crazy. Plus, she needed advice. Who wants to take advice from a crazy person?

"How's your arm, Mary? Do you need to see Doc this morning?"

She lifted her arm in response. "No, it's fine." She still couldn't believe her luck at being alive today. She turned her gaze back to the room. "This is a lot of cookies for one day. Do your employees buy this many every day?"

Mrs. Klaus retrieved two glasses from a cabinet and placed them on the table. She walked to the fridge and pulled out a pitcher of milk. She arranged cookies on a plate and set them at the end of her large work station.

"Have a seat, my dear."

"Thank you." She chose a stool next to the table.

Joy sat beside her.

She crammed a cookie in her mouth, and her tongue did a happy dance. *Oh my gosh.* They were as good as the ones she'd eaten on the first day. Maybe better. "Delicious," she mumbled with a mouth full of awesomeness.

Mrs. Klaus blushed. "Thank you. I'm not as good as our regular baker, but I try."

Mary shook her head. "Seriously. That cookie was the best I've ever eaten."

"Thank you. The recipe has been in our family for centuries."

Mrs. Klaus had ignored Mary's earlier question. Mary didn't have time to play North Pole detective. Her life stewed in a total state of chaos.

"What is the emergency, Mary? Norman said it was important."

Mary's eyelids dropped. "I'm confused. Mrs. Klaus, I'm so confused." She stood and began pacing. "You see, the rekindling thing worked...but..."

"That's wonderful news." Mrs. Klaus tried to look surprised, but Mary knew she wasn't.

"You see, that's the problem. What's so wonderful about it?" Mary didn't give her a chance to respond. "I mean the passion is there...wow...is it there." Her cheeks warmed. "I mean passion was never our problem, even though now...wow." Her hand flew over her mouth and she looked into Joy's eyes. "I'm sorry. I don't know why I keep saying that."

Mrs. Klaus giggled. "It's okay, my dear."

Sure easy for you to say. You didn't just blurt out your sex life to Santa's wife. "I guess what I mean is that even though things are great now, we haven't dealt with all the problems that brought us here in the first place." She threw her hands up. "In fact, we've just totally complicated things."

Mrs. Klaus listened to Mary's rant in silence.

"Don't you see? My divorce will be final in two weeks. This wasn't supposed to happen. I can't let JT take me for granted again. I can't go back to being the wife who sits alone and forgotten." As soon as the words left her lips, relief sored through her. There her fears were, out in the open. What she'd worried about since the recent make-up.

Mrs. Klaus stood and returned her attention to the bowl of batter. "Do you still wish to be divorced?"

Mary collapsed back on her stool. "I don't know. I know I was scared to death during and after the accident. I know I wanted and needed JT more than I've ever wanted and needed him before. But just because we fanned the old passion flame, nothing substantial has changed." Her words trailed off in a whisper. Her gaze locked with Joy's. "He still left me at the airport alone. I went on our anniversary vacation...alone. He still loves his job above all things." Tears burned her eyes. "And that includes me."

"Were you happy yesterday, when you and JT rekindled your lost passion?"

"Very."

"It seems your happiness didn't last very long."

Mary met Joy's compassionate gaze. "You see. That's the thing." She ran a hand through her hair. "I don't trust happiness."

Silence filled the room.

"Mary. May I ask you a question without upsetting you?" Mrs. Klaus set aside her wooden spoon and folded her hands in front of her.

Why do people ask permission to upset you? That question always comes with some sort of blow.

Mary hesitated before nodding.

"Do you take any responsibility for the fall of your marriage?"

What? Me? Mary's defense sensor kicked into full throttle. She jumped up and started to pace once more. She'd been a great wife. She'd done everything expected. She cooked. She cleaned.

"Being a good maid isn't the qualifications for making a great wife."

Mary's head jerked in Joy's direction. How did she read her mind so easily? She crossed her arms and lifted her chin. "I was very good to my husband."

Guilt punched her in the stomach. She'd been a good wife. Sometimes. But she nagged JT constantly about Whitney Conner. Didn't trust him when he swore he wanted nothing to do with her. Scared every time they'd disagree on something, he'd pack up and leave. Refused to have children, afraid if the marriage ended the child would carry the undeserved burden of responsibility. Anger churned her stomach.

Why did Mrs. Klaus ask her such a personal question in the first place? She said that wasn't the way they operated here.

"I'm sorry, Mary. I'm afraid I've touched on a delicate subject."

You bet you have. But in Mrs. Klaus' defense, she'd asked for it.

Joy Klaus forced a flat smile. She opened a drawer and retrieved another apron. "How about you and I bake some cookies?"

How in the Santa-la-la-la would baking cookies help? Her life had become more screwed up than ever, and Joy Klaus wanted to bake cookies. Mary released the deep breath she'd been holding and tossed another cookie in her mouth. Oh, well. Better than being put under the magnifying glass.

****

JT walked all over town searching for his wife. Instead of Mary, he found Norman at Rudolph's Big and Small Shop. He stood before a mirror wearing a red button-down shirt, green pants, and a holly print bow tie.

Yikes.

"What do you think?" Norman examined his reflection.

JT held back a chuckle. He looked like Christmas over-done. But then again, this wasn't your normal fashion kind of town. So he lied. "Sharp, dude. You look sharp."

"I hope Missy thinks so."

"She'll be chasing you under the mistletoe in no time wearing that get-up."

Norman's cheeks turned the shade of his overly bright shirt. Then he slipped in to the dressing room to change.

"How about we grab some lunch?" Norman said after he paid for his purchase.

JT checked his watch. He really wanted to have lunch with Mary, but she was nowhere to be found. What if she'd skipped out?

"Mrs. Walker's helping Mrs. K at the factory."

He was convinced his new little friend could read minds. But the information did put JT at ease. Mary hadn't taken off, at least.

****

JT climbed the steps of the inn an hour later, wondering if Mary had made it back yet.

"Joseph. How are you, son?"

Nick's voice called JT's attention to one of the rockers on the porch. A pipe hung from his lips, with a trail of gray smoke lingering in the air around him.

JT joined him. "I would have never guessed you for a smoker."

Nick took the pipe from his mouth and smiled. "Mrs. Klaus has been trying to get me to quit for centuries." He winked. "But we must stick to tradition."

The stump of a pipe he held tight in his teeth, and the smoke it encircled his head like a wreath.

That came from nowhere. JT hadn't heard the Christmas poem since he was a kid.

"I heard you and the missus are doing well." Nick ended with his low *ho-ho-ho* laugh.

JT arched a brow. "I guess."

Nick blew out a ring of gray smoke. "Is this skepticism I hear in your voice?"

JT leaned back in his rocker and clutched his hands around the end of the arms. "I mean, some things are great. Perfect. But we're here—now." He looked at Nick. "We haven't really solved any of the issues that brought us to the inn in the first place."

Nick's rocker creaked over the porch boards. "Sometimes things have a way of working themselves out once the love resurfaces."

"You don't know Mary. She over-analyzes everything. She'll want to rehash the whole kit and caboodle." He sighed. "But to be honest, I can't blame

146

her. I was a real jackass in the past."

"Example?"

JT peered over the rail at the sun setting behind the mountains. *Heck. Where do I start?* "Let's see, I work too much. In fact, I put work above everything."

"Reason?"

JT glanced at Nick, a little irritated with his one word questions. Nick puffed on his pipe, staring at the town before him.

"My old man always pressured me to be the best at everything. I had a 3.9 GPA in high school, but my grades weren't good enough. I made MVP every year in football, but because I didn't get drafted by the pros, I wasn't good enough." JT rocked his chair a little too fast. "When I decided to be an engineering contractor, he about had a cow. He wanted a doctor or lawyer."

Dorky David came to mind and his hand knotted into a fist.

"Once Dad finally got on board with my career choice, he made me shoot for the sky. Couldn't build decks or even houses. I needed to go for skyscrapers." He glanced at Nick. "Don't get me wrong. I love building skyscrapers. And not to sound pompous, I'm pretty darn good at it. I make great money, and I have a reputation of being the best around." He leaned back and crossed his legs at his ankles. "But taking my dad's advice and being the best has landed me on the edge of a big fat divorce."

Nick sat silently. Only the occasional sound of him sucking on his pipe broke the quiet.

JT sighed. "When I got married, I got the same lecture. Now you're a husband and maybe one day a father. Succeed. Succeed. Succeed." He wasn't sure why he shared all this with Nick. "So, I guess I took him literally. I may be the best at my job, but I suck as a husband."

Nick stopped rocking. "Young man. I usually don't go around contradicting fathers, but I think in this case, yours has missed the true meaning of life."

He turned his head. "And what in the world would that be?" *Please enlighten me.*

"You don't have to be the best. Just try really hard to be good."

JT snorted. *Did the whole point of life come down to the good versus naughty list?*

"You need balance. Be a good employee. A good employer. Be a good son. Be a good husband. A good father. But most importantly be good to Joseph Tanner Walker."

Nick took a quick puff off his pipe. "JT, before you can be good to someone else, you must first be good to yourself."

His shoulders slumped. Quite deep coming from *Santa Claus.*

"Nick, how do you know which one is most important? Which one should get the most attention?

"Let me put it like this. When you started building the Jefferson Tower, did you build the walls first?"

JT wasn't even going to ask how he knew about the Jefferson Tower. That building cost him his marriage. "Of course not. You start with the foundation."

Nick grinned. "Think of your life as a building." He put his weathered hand on the arm of JT's rocker. "Your marriage being the foundation." Nick sighed. "Son, you must keep balance in all areas of your life.'

He turned his bushy eyebrows toward JT. "What do you think is the most important thing in an office building? Electrical or plumbing?"

"They're both equally important."

"Walls or roof?" Nick's expression was hard to read.

"Both."

"My point exactly. Consider your marriage the foundation of your life. Your parents the roof, your career the walls, your friends the plumbing." Nick raised a brow. "You get my point. If you build only walls without a foundation, where would that leave you?"

"Two weeks from being divorced."

Nick winked, and a grin slid across his puffy cheeks. "A lot can happen in a week or two."

"In the meantime, how do I get Mary to forget about me ditching her on her surprise anniversary trip?" JT winced. He'd hurt her beyond repair that day.

"Did you ever tell her about Mr. Daniels?"

JT shot Nick a curious stare. How did he know about that? Mary had it right. What the Klauses knew amounted to borderline creepy.

"I think Mary is a compassionate person. She never got to hear your side of the story. It could have changed everything."

JT shook his head and stood. He leaned against the rail and braced his palms on the cool wood. "No, Nick. I think this is where I'll have to disagree with you. Mr. Daniels didn't cause me to miss the plane. My screwed up priorities did that."

"What excuse did you give for missing the plane?"

JT shook his head. "I didn't. She'd left me a

message, telling me to get the hell out." He stared down at the railing. "So I did. By the time she returned from the trip, I had moved out."

"JT, why didn't you fly out the next day?"

He considered for a brief second that Nick already knew the answer. "It was a surprise, remember. Mary made all the reservations." He shrugged. "I didn't know where the hell to fly to." He ran a hand through his dark hair. "Nick, I've made so many mistakes. And missing the plane was the biggest."

Nick stood and patted JT's shoulder. "Joseph, there are no mistakes. You were exactly where you were supposed to be that day. Just as you are exactly where you are supposed to be today."

Chapter 11

Happiness.

Mary read the morning theme card, then tapped it against her palm. *Easy for you to say, Mrs. Klaus.* She was ninety percent ecstatic with the recent change of events. But ten percent of her still wallowed in the land of *what happens when?*

What happens when they leave the Rekindle Inn and get back to the real world? What happens when JT goes back to work? A punch of guilt stung her middle, turning her stomach into a tangled mess. What happens when she tells David the brief relationship they shared was over? She hated hurting him. But it had to be done. *Wow.* The *I told you so* he'd throw in her face wouldn't be fun.

Happiness. Right. Mary tossed the card on the table.

She smiled, so widely it hurt her cheeks. JT had succeeded in making her happy last night. Three times in fact. Warmth covered her cheeks. The last few days with him had been unbelievable. Maybe she didn't have all the answers, but she did have twenty-four hours left of her magical vacation. She sure wouldn't spend the time moping because of her nonstop fear of happiness.

The day's schedule didn't leave her much time for worry. They'd be busy for hours. Breakfast with the Klauses. Ice sculpting in the park. Another sleigh ride in the afternoon. Then the Christmas Barn Dance in the evening.

*****

Mary prepared to descend the steps of the inn when JT grabbed her hand, pulling her into his arms. Her arms slid around his neck as he wrapped his around her waist.

"Mary, I know you don't want to talk about the past right now."

"We're not allowed, remember? Mrs. Klaus has strict rules about that." *Plus, why take a chance on ruining the happiness?* She searched his blue eyes and her heart warmed when she saw love reflecting back. She wasn't ready to lose *this*. This magic.

Before he had a chance to speak again, she stretched on her tiptoes and kissed him. If his mouth was busy, he couldn't talk.

He returned her kiss but then pulled back. "Let me just say one thing."

Her shoulders slumped and her head fell to his shoulder. "Why? We can talk tomorrow on the way home."

He cupped her face and forced her to look at him.

Here we go.

He grinned. "I just want to say one thing." He kissed the end of her nose.

"Fine. One thing." She sighed and waited for the bomb to drop and explode on *Happiness* day.

His dark blue eyes softened. "I just want to tell you, I'll never hurt you again. I promise."

A sharp pain speared her chest. What a big promise to keep. She brushed her finger over his face, outlining his strong cheek bones. She knew he believed his

152

declaration. But she also knew it as an impossible promise to keep. Her gaze locked with his dark blue eyes, and her heart swelled. The magic three little words danced around her tongue, but she refused to voice them. Not yet. So she settled for, "Okay."

His lips curved, and his lids narrowed. He pressed his mouth against hers.

****

"How's your arm this morning, Mary?" Joy Klaus took the last bite of her scrambled eggs.

Mary lifted her arm. "It's fine. I'm not having any pain today."

Amazing. JT wasn't sure what Doc did to her wound, but she moved her arm with ease. His stomach knotted when he remembered tending to the cut after the accident. Talking about nasty. He thought the cut would need about a hundred stitches.

"Doc is a miracle worker." Nick raised his brows.

No doubt. Miracle is right. There was no way Mary should be moving her arm the way she did without a *miracle.*

The waitress came and cleared their plates. JT wanted to say something to his hosts, but words deserted him.

"The two of you have a busy day ahead. Are you up for it, Mary?"

Mary turned to JT and smiled. "Looking forward to it."

He leaned in and brushed a kiss on the top of her head. "Me, too."

"Then we'll let you get to it." Nick moved to stand.

"Nick, if you can wait a second."

Nick settled back in his chair.

Once JT had everyone's attention, he searched for the right words. "You could say when we came here a few days ago, I came for all the wrong reasons." He turned a shameful gaze toward his wife before he settled back on the inn's owners. "I didn't have any expectations your techniques would work. In fact, I guess you could say I considered them a little odd and corny."

He glanced sheepishly from one Klaus to another.

"But I was so wrong. Somehow forcing us to go back in time and searching our hearts for the love…" He sighed. This was coming out all wrong. "I guess I just wanted to thank you. Thank you for helping us save our marriage. Thank you for caring about us." JT squeezed his wife's hand, and when he met her gaze, her eyes were glassy.

Mrs. Klaus placed a soft hand over JT's. "True love like yours doesn't come along very often." Her sentimental gaze darted between his and Mary's. "We are just glad to be a part of it."

Awkward silence fell over the table.

Okay. Didn't mean to make this weird. When did he become so…mushy?

"Ho, ho, ho!" Nick bellowed. "Who's up for a little ice sculpting?"

JT grinned and turned to his wife. "Let's go make beautiful ice together."

****

The competition was being held in the park. Looked to be about eight couples all together. Each couple had a designated block of ice that stood about six feet tall. JT gripped a small chainsaw in his hands as he waited for Nick to blow the start whistle.

"Do you have any idea what we're going to make?" Mary asked eyeing the icepick and ice-saw she held in each hand.

"Nope. You got any ideas?"

Mary's lips thinned and she raised a brow. "We need to do something unique."

JT looked over Mary's shoulder at the snow-covered Christmas tree. "How about the tree? We'd have a model to go by."

Mary glanced over her shoulder. "Perfect."

"I'll get the basic shape with the chainsaw, then we can put in the details with the hand tools."

Mary's blue eyes lit and excitement danced across her pretty face. The pressure was on. JT didn't know the first thing about how to create a Christmas tree out of ice, but he'd give it his best shot. He had to impress Mary.

Nick blew his whistle and JT yanked on the chainsaw cable. The motor roared, and he jumped into action. He started at the top and worked his way down. Zipping the blade this way and zagging it the other. Leaving Mary blinded by streams of flying ice chips.

"Hey. Watch it," Mary yelled, followed by a shriek of laughter.

Even with the freezing temperatures, he was warm all over. Watching her blew his mind. She literally glowed. He knew why. She appeared free. Free from worry and stress. She looked like a different person from the Mary he'd met up with a couple of weeks ago at O'Malley's.

"Watch out," Mary shouted and pointed to the block of ice.

JT turned and watched in horror as a big chunk of

ice fell to the ground. *Crap.* Guess this tree would have a missing limb or two.

"Sorry." He grinned. "You're distracting me."

"Me?"

They locked gazes.

"Why?"

JT shut off his saw and placed it on the ground. "Because you're so damn beautiful."

Mary's cheeks turned red, and her gaze fell to the ground.

****

Mary knew she blushed. She could feel the heat in her face. She'd gotten used to the silly girlish reaction. Oh well. When a girl had a guy as hot as JT looking her over all the time, what was she supposed to do?

"You gave our tree a bare spot."

JT grimaced and stared at the ice. "Yep. I see that."

"What are you going to do about it?" Mary teased.

He tossed his hands on his sides. "I'm not sure." His eyes met hers. "Any suggestions?"

She nibbled on her bottom lip to keep from laughing. "I guess if Charlie Brown can turn a tree with fifteen pine needles into something beautiful, we should be able to do something with two-thirds of a demolished tree."

"Demolished?" His eyes widened. "A little harsh, don't you think? I'd say injured."

She laughed. "Injured?" She shook her head. "Then you need to call for Doc because your tree is in desperate need of CPR."

They spent the next hour shaping their partially damaged tree into something beautiful. She worked hard creating ornaments, while he smoothed the ice branches.

Wow. They made a pretty good team after all. He'd been working hard on a section in the rear of the tree for a few minutes now.

"What are you doing back there?"

He grinned. "You'll see."

Nick blew the whistle. "Okay folks, tools down."

She stepped back to get a better look. *Not bad.* The missing chunk of ice didn't even seem noticeable now. *Well, maybe a little.*

"How's it look?" He joined her.

Her heart warmed as her eyes moved over the ice tree. "Perfect." It was, too. They'd taken something blank and cold and created something special. Just as the Rekindle Inn had done for them. Their relationship had turned into a block of frozen ice. Hard. Cold. Detached.

Mary circled the tree. She stopped when she noticed JT's recent project. He'd carved replicas of the ornaments they'd made their first day at the inn.

Her glance lifted and she met his gaze. "That's so sweet."

His lips turned upward, and he shrugged a shoulder. "That's me. Sweet."

Yeah, right. Mary swooped down and grabbed a handful of snow. She balled it in her fist before he had a chance to figure out her actions, then launched it at him. His eyes widened as he stared down at the round, white mark on his chest.

"Oh, it's on now." He bent down to snatch up his own snow.

Oh, shoot. What have I done? Run. She sprinted as fast as she could through the park when a hard thump hit her in the shoulder. She turned and saw him approaching fast. Oh, no. She couldn't stop the giggle from escaping her lips. Strong arms wrapped around her waist causing her to stumble. Their bodies fell against the ground and she rolled in the snow, until she came to rest on her back. JT's large frame settled on top of her.

His dark blue gaze scanned her face. "You okay?"

She didn't speak. Just nodded her head. She licked at her dry lips, and his gaze lingered on her mouth. His long dark lashes shadowed his face, and she melted into the warmth of his stare. He leaned in and pressed his mouth against hers.

Mary's mind whirled in the passion and beauty of the kiss. She knew this was a unique moment, a gift in time that would remain with her always. Unlike any moment before, and any moment after.

When JT's mouth lifted from hers, she opened her eyes. His stare sent her belly into a spin of yearning. Yearning for him. Yearning for hope. Yearning for healing for her broken marriage.

"I love you, Mary."

Before she could stop the words, they tumbled from her mouth. "I love you, too." There it was. Out in the world. Vulnerability hovered over her, leaving her unsure and exposed.

His face brightened. "I'll be your hero again one day. I promise."

Mary wanted to believe him. She wanted to believe in *happiness* like the card suggested. But happiness could be sneaky and cruel. Happiness wrapped you in its arms of trust and love, soaring you to the highest mountain of contentment. Then when everything felt safe, *happiness* dropped you from the sky, sending you crashing to the hard ground beneath, shattering your heart into thousands of little pieces. Impossible to put back together.

****

Mary waited with JT later in the afternoon for the sleigh to pick them up.

"You've been awfully quiet since the snowball fight. Did I hurt your arm when we fell?"

She turned to her husband. His eyes were filled with worry. She knew the look. She shook her head. "No. My arm's fine."

He sighed, stuck his hands in his pockets and looked away. Mary didn't fool him. It was obvious. She'd retreated since the big *I love you* declaration between the two of them. Now would probably be a good time to say something reassuring, but she had nothing.

Stop thinking so much. Good grief. She was Debbie Downer on depressants. *Just enjoy this moment and every moment until this crazy vacation ends. Heck. There'll be plenty of time for self-destruction after we leave tinsel-town.*

Then the little nagging elf on her shoulder shelf, whispered, *Or you could go off by yourself. The chances of this romantic ride getting a little deep is a no-brainer. Do you really want that?*

Norman arrived in the nick of time. Mary and JT snuggled in tightly under the warm blanket. JT leaned in with dark eyes, and as she got lost in his blue stare, she was happy. At least for now.

Shut up, elf.

****

Mary slid the red lipstick over her lips. A little brighter than she normally wore, but tonight was the Christmas dance. She wore a cream sweater dress gathered at the waist with a leather belt and her favorite brown boots. The dance was being held in a barn, so stilettos were out of the question.

Her eyes settled on her reflection. She pressed a palm to her rosy cheek. She was in love. In love with her husband. A man she'd loathed with all of her being just a week before.

Holy Christmas tree. Life was complicated. She resisted the urge to chew on her bottom lip. Didn't want to smudge her lipstick. But her newfound glow was shadowed by a dark gray cloud overhead. Weighted down with the moisture of uncertainty. What would happen tomorrow when this magical vacation ended? She folded her arms firmly around her. The familiar sound of doubt echoed in her brain. If only she could stop talking herself out of happiness. But she had mastered that craft.

Why'd you fall for him again? Why did you come in the first place?

The heart-twisting agony of losing JT had started to heal. At least the pain had become numb.

Mary's lids closed. He was there. She didn't have to turn around to know he stood watching her. But she did anyway. The second their gazes met, she knew why she'd come. Her heart reminded her why. Because she loved JT to the moon and back. She wished she didn't, but she did. He smiled, and her heart did a cartwheel. He leaned against the doorframe. His arms were crossed over his chest. Tall, strong and overly handsome.

"Wow. You look fantastic."

She blushed at his compliment like the high school girl he'd turned her into.

"Thanks."

He reached for her. He brought her hand to his lips and kissed the inside of her wrist. *Now what?*

A knock came at the door. *Thank goodness.* Her mind needed a rest from unanswerable questions. Norman rushed in carrying a silver tray containing a bucket of champagne and two crystal flutes. His bright green and red outfit was...*very* festive. Mary covered her mouth to hide her giggle.

"Compliments of the inn." He dropped the tray on the table, then left as quickly as he'd come. "See you folks in thirty minutes."

JT's brows arched. "That's what I'm talking about." He picked up the bottle and peeled away the gold wrapper. He popped the top, and bubbles oozed down the sides. A laugh roared out of him. A cheerful laugh. Mary had forgotten how much she loved the sound.

He filled the glasses and slid the bottle back into the ice. He handed her a glass and when his fingers brushed over hers, excitement clouded her senses.

Just from a touch. *Good grief.* Face it. She was done for.

He tilted his glass in her direction. "To the wackiest, greatest little town I know."

She smiled, and they dinged glasses.

"For sure." She hesitated before taking a sip. "And to rekindling the love I believed was lost forever." Yes. She loved him. She never stopped loving him.

JT's lips thinned. "Cheers."

Her eyes had revealed too much. *God.* Where were they headed? She wasn't sure, but she knew she didn't want to let him go. Not again. Her heart wouldn't take it.

She brought the glass to her lips and took a deep swallow.

"I love you." His words warmed her more than the champagne. He set his glass down and reached for her. "Mary, there's so much to say. So much needs to be said."

"I know." She shook her head. "But can't it wait? I want to live in the magic. In this moment, right here in Jollyville." She rubbed her palm down the side of his cheek. "This is our last night. Let's suck up every moment here, while we're able."

Chicken. She knew it. But she couldn't take the chance of talking and having all the ugliness return. Her heart rejoiced. Finally, after a really long time, she'd become the most important thing in JT's life. She wouldn't give that up.

His features softened.

He knew the rules. No talking about their problems. She searched his eyes for understanding.

"Please." She begged. "I promise we'll talk later." She rested her cheek against his broad chest. "Not now, JT. Please." The room quieted, only the comforting sound of his heartbeat sounded in her ear. "Besides, we signed the stupid commitment agreement. No discussing the past while we're here."

"Yep. I guess we did." He kissed her hair, then rested his chin on the top of her head. Holding her tight as if she were a life vest in a raging ocean.

"I love you, babe."

God, she hoped so.

****

They walked along the path arm in arm. They'd almost reached the barn when he tugged her to a halt.

"Hold on a sec."

She stopped. "Is everything okay?" When she looked at JT, he held a small box wrapped in gold paper with a shiny red ribbon in his hand. Her heart thumped.

"Merry Christmas."

Her cheeks warmed. She hadn't gotten him a present. Jerk alert. "I didn't…"

"Shhh." He pushed the present toward her. "It's just a little something to remember the time we've spent here together."

Her gaze darted to his. *Shoot.* He worried, too. He thought they'd blow it once they left Christmasville.

"Mary. Please. It's not a big deal. Open it." He nudged it against her hand.

She took the box. Almost too pretty to open. She unwrapped the present. A beautiful necklace with a heart-shaped ruby outlined in diamonds glistened up at her. "JT." Her fingers fanned over her chest. "It's beautiful."

"Just like my wife." He took the necklace from her shaking hands and slipped it around her neck, fastening it in the back.

Her fingers found the stone, and she clasped it in her hand. "Thank you."

He brushed a kiss against her forehead. "Now. You ready to get your dance on?"

Mary glanced toward the huge red barn. "I'm thinking more like square dance on."

Chapter 12

The barn had been transformed into a magical Christmas wonderland. A million white lights twinkled from the rafters. Garland draped from the hayloft all around the beams. Support columns were wrapped with pine boughs and ribbon. Red covered tables sat neatly off to the sides loaded with food and drinks. The space was huge. Big enough for all the animals in the forest to live comfortably.

"Wow. They really go all out." JT slipped his fingers in Mary's and led her through the huge doorways.

A band blasted "Run Run Rudolf" from a make-shift stage to the right.

"This is unbelievable," she shouted over the music. JT squeezed her fingers. The strange tingling sensation was back. This time, both love and joy overtook her senses, leaving a trail of goose bumps along her spine. Magic was definitely in the air.

Grinning from ear to ear, Norman greeted JT with a fist bump. Mary rolled her eyes.

"Welcome to our annual barn dance." His attitude was almost childlike. Mr. and Mrs. Klaus waved to them from across the room. "There's plenty of food." His eyebrow arched, and he leaned in to reveal some big secret. "Scrooge even has some green beer in the back." He threw his thumb over his shoulder.

They looked in that direction to find Marley Scrooge. He nodded and held a red plastic cup in the air.

"This time keep the peppermint stick."

JT laughed. "You know it."

JT met her gaze. "You want to go mingle or get something to eat?"

"Actually a green beer is sounding pretty good right now."

He grinned. "That's my girl."

It was their last night, and she wanted to make every second count. Starting with Marley's beer.

"Okay. Here we go." He smiled as they took a taste of peppermint stick beer together.

She shrugged a shoulder. "Not bad." *Not gross at all.* The next item on the agenda was JT's advice to Norman on dating. Some hoop-la about being confident and taking charge. She leaned against the wall and nursed her beer. Resisting the temptation to put in her two cents.

The band struck up a slow song.

"Okay, dude. This is the perfect opportunity to go ask Missy to dance."

Norman turned a bright shade of red. "I can't do it, dude."

She arched a brow. *Dude.* The universal man name.

"Yes, you can. Watch a professional." JT reached for her hand. "Mary, can I make every man here jealous, by dancing with the most beautiful woman in the room?"

"Sure." She turned to Norman. "See. His line is so pathetic I actually feel sorry for him," she joked and let JT lead her toward the dance floor.

He turned to Norman and winked. "See, dude. Works every time." When they reached the dance floor, he pulled her against him, and her arms slid around his neck. They swayed to the music. The soothing rhythm of his heartbeat against her ear calmed the rising panic. The last night in a town where magic did exist.

Once the magic was gone, then what?

She'd forgotten how wonderful it was to be nestled in his strong arms. She wanted the dance to go on forever.

He whispered in her ear, and the warmth of his breath almost made her miss a step. "Does it seem everyone is extra happy tonight?"

Mary glanced around. Townspeople were smiling at her from every direction. Yes. They did seem…happier. Deloris from the Peppermint Café looked the happiest of all. She seemed about to swing her arm out of its socket with her crazy wave. Wearing a giant smile, along with a retro-chic red poodle skirt. Mary returned the greeting. *Good grief.* Green beer must be flowing through the crowd.

Mary nibbled on her bottom lip, trying to make sense of the extra jollyful Jollyvillians. *Duh.* "I know why everyone's so happy."

"Spiked egg nog?"

She shook her head. "No. The town's celebrating."

He stared at her. "It is a Christmas party."

"Don't you see? The Rekindle Inn was a success. They're celebrating us *rekindling* our love."

He glanced over her shoulder. His gaze moved over the room. "Wow. You're right. Everyone *is* watching us." He pulled her in tighter. A naughty smile stretched across his entire face.

She looked up. "What?"

"I'm just thinking I'm going to hit it big on the Santa drop this year."

Mary laughed. "Glad I could be of help."

He lifted her in the air and twirled her around. She squealed even louder. She was happy. Truly happy.

They took a break after the song ended and moved to the refreshment table. She moved the food on her plate around with a plastic fork. For some odd reason, David's face flashed in her mind. Funny. She hadn't missed David at all. He was a wonderful person, but no other man stood a chance with her. How could they when the one sitting beside her had never let her go?

JT moved out those few months ago, without a word. He didn't defend his actions for missing the plane, nor stand up for her and the marriage. He said nothing. Nothing. He just left. They'd only communicated through text and voicemails ever since. Or lawyers. Not that defending himself would have done any good.

He'd broken her trust. He would've been wasting his time.

"Mary."

JT stared at her. "You okay?"

She nodded. What made her thoughts go to such a dreadful place? The past. Maybe because tomorrow they would be back in Virginia without the dome of magic protecting their marriage. That's what.

"Well, I'll be darned?" JT's tone was low.

She followed his gaze. Norman and Missy stood across the room holding hands. Both as red as the stripe on a candy cane. Mary smiled. Young love. What a great feeling. She'd experienced a little of it herself lately.

The night flew with one dance after another. Mingling with the folks of Jollyville and the Klauses of course. She thought it a bittersweet evening. An unsolicited yawn escaped her.

No. She didn't want to be tired.

Mary didn't want this to be their last night. She didn't want to leave. Couldn't they just stay here, get jobs and never go back to the real world?

Mary turned toward JT as he brought the hand he'd been holding up to his lips and kissed it.

"How about I take you home?"

She sensed her blush instantly. Home. Wouldn't that be a welcome Christmas present? But she was pretty sure he meant the inn. Even though the thought of being alone with him there had her insides soaring like Santa's reindeer on a Christmas Eve flight.

She nodded. They said their goodbyes. An emptiness filled her heart when she realized she might never see some of these people again.

Deloris almost squeezed her to death. "We are so glad you folks came up here and let us fix you."

Well, temporarily anyway.

"We knew you two were special," she continued. "Sant—Mr. Klaus always knows." She blushed. "He has a way about these things."

Mary had stopped thinking of the townsfolk as crazy. Unusual, yes, but the love and kindness overshadowed all else. They waved to Norman and his new girl twirling around the dance floor. He waved cheerfully back.

A horse-drawn sleigh waited for them when they walked out. The driver jumped down from his perch and helped them in.

"How about one last trip around town?" the man asked as she and JT nestled under the blanket.

"Sounds perfect." She smiled into her husband's eyes. This sleigh ride was the polar opposite from the first one. The first time she strained her back trying not to touch JT. This time it was as if their two separate bodies had molded into one. The moon illuminated the white covered hills and valleys with sparkles. Trees shadowed the mountains, and the horse's bells echoed through the town, sending her into a state of euphoria. She would have never guessed in a million years so much could change in one week.

JT slipped his thumb under her chin, and she looked into his shadowed face with eager anticipation. As his face slowly tilted toward hers, everything around them vanished. His warm breath brushed against her mouth. His lips pressed gently against hers, and her head twirled with passion. How could one gentle kiss speak a thousand unsaid words?

What would happen tomorrow when their plane landed back in Virginia? She didn't want to think about that now. She couldn't. The sleigh pulled up to the inn, and they bolted from it. The driver laughed his goodbye as they raced up the steps two at a time.

He took her hand and dragged her up the three flights of stairs. They were winded when they reached the hallway to their room, but he still had enough strength to push her against the wall and ravish her mouth, ear, the side of her neck. Her throat. Down to the vee of her dress.

Room. Room.

They needed the room now. She jerked free and

ran the few steps to the door. Yanking the key from her pocket she unlocked it and slung it open.

JT swept her into his arms and carried her over the threshold. Mary squealed. She kicked the door closed with her foot and let him carry her to the bedroom. Once he sat her down, she was like a mad woman, ripping his shirt open with one hard tug. Buttons flew and scattered on the floor. She wanted to see his glorious body, feel every strong muscle beneath her touch. She leaned in and kissed his bare chest, exploring his build with her fingers. Mary's hand moved downward until she felt the stiffness of his erection pressed against it, causing her insides to yearn for what was about to happen.

The rest was a big fiery blur of passion and bodies entwined for hours. They never spoke a word. They didn't need to. Emotions lay scattered all around them. The regret of past hurts. Fear of the future. Love. So much love. They held onto each other and didn't let go. Not until the sun rose through the windows early the next morning. She pressed her eyes shut against the morning light. Wishing time to stand still. Scared for what would happen when they left the magical ambiance of the Rekindle Inn.

Chapter 13

JT sat in Mrs. Klaus' office and watched as she took the three keys and unlocked the safe. She handed them their belongings. He slid his phone in his pocket along with his other things. He had Joy put all charges on his card. He'd miss this place.

When they completed their final transaction, Mary hugged the woman tightly as they said their goodbyes. He didn't want to interrupt or rush the ladies as they talked.

"I'm going to look for Norman. I'd like to tell him goodbye before we leave."

Mary smiled leaving JT's heart pounding. God, she was beautiful. Her long blonde hair cascaded around her shoulders. Her blue eyes were bursting with what he hoped was happiness. She nodded, and he turned and headed out to the porch.

Their luggage was stacked neatly on the sidewalk ready to be loaded in Nick's old truck parked out front. No sign of Norman. A shiny new Jaguar sat behind the pickup looking very out of place.

"So, you must be JT?"

JT jerked around to see who asked. He didn't need introductions, he knew who the uptight guy in the suit and wool overcoat must be. Dorky David.

"What the hell are you doing here?"

David's expression hardened. "I'm here to get my

fiancée. She called saying this week was one big mistake. She asked me to drive up here and get her as soon as I could."

No. He had to be lying.

"I'm sorry, I don't remember Mary mentioning that." JT's stomach ached like he'd been sucker punched.

"Which part?"

David pulled a small box from his pocket and popped the top, revealing the biggest diamond ring JT had ever seen. *Damn.*

"Dude, you need to get back in that overpriced car and go back to where you came from," JT said, pointing a stern finger toward the Jag. "The only mistake that's been made here is you showing up on my vacation."

David laughed. JT had never wanted to punch someone in the mouth as much as he wanted to punch the smirk off this guy's face. It was as if JT's collar had shrunk to ten sizes too small, strangling the air he breathed. This guy needed to go before Mary came out and saw the ginormous ring and forget all about rekindling things with her husband.

"Afraid not, *dude*. Not without Mary."

JT took a step toward him, but Mary came flying out of the inn with her phone stretched out in front of her. "JT, what is this?" Her eyes screamed panic, and she hadn't even noticed David yet.

She didn't wait for him to speak. "We got our phones mixed up." Her hand shook as she held it out to him. "You said you hadn't seen Whitney on a personal level. Apparently she's been trying to reach you. A lot." Tears welled up in her eyes. "You lied. Why would you lie? It's not like we were together."

JT took the phone and read the text displayed on the screen.

JT, I forgot how good we are together. Get your ass back from that lame vacation so we can do it again.

No way. This. Was. Not. Happening. This would send Mary and her trust issues back about a thousand years. He took Mary's phone out of his pocket and she yanked it out of his hand.

"Mary. God, I missed you."

Mary turned to see David standing behind her. Her face paled. Yep. Their second chance had ended. Things were melting away as rapidly as the snow on the sun-covered mountain. JT needed a redo. He wanted to take Mary back in the inn and start this day over. Now.

"David. What are you doing here?"

David looked offended by her apparent lack of excitement, but only for a second. He plastered, what JT was sure was a practiced lawyer smile, on his face.

"I came to get you, snookums."

Oh, God. Seriously? JT would puke if he heard more of that.

Mary stared blankly for a second, then her gaze darted back to JT. "Well?"

JT knew he needed to say something. He needed to say something good. But instead he stood there.

In silence.

"JT, say something?"

Say what. That Whitney Conner is a crazy stalker? Why? He knew Mary wouldn't believe him. Just like she never believed him when he assured her a thousand times she was the most important thing in his life, not his job. He knew they'd have their challenges when they got back home, but damn, they hadn't even left the porch.

"There is nothing to say," David answered for him. "It's obvious he doesn't have anything to say. Let the piece of garbage go. He never deserved you in the first place."

Mary's stare never left JT's.

JT wasn't sure if it was the doubt he saw in Mary's eyes or the confidence he saw in David's that kept him mute. But he knew one thing for sure. He wouldn't stand there and try to explain himself with lawyer boy as an audience. So he did what every stupid, prideful man would do. He grabbed his bag and made his way down the steps without a word. He tossed his bag in the back of Nick's truck and climbed in the seat.

Nick hollered out to Mary. "Mrs. Walker, you ready to go?"

Mary shook her head. "No. Go without me."

It would have hurt less if Santa's eight reindeer had run JT down. Their marriage was over. Again.

****

Nick didn't say anything for a good twenty miles. "I'm sorry, JT. We are usually pretty good at keeping outsiders out. But it seems Norman didn't show up for his duties this morning."

JT glanced at him, a little confused.

"You could say he's head of security along with a few other things."

"Oh." JT sighed. "It's not Norman's fault. It was bound to happen sooner or later."

Nick grasped the steering wheel a little tighter. "Regardless, Norman should have been on duty." Nick tsked. "Something tells me that young man may find himself on the naughty list."

JT couldn't help but snicker. Even with his own life falling apart, JT was happy for Norman. The little dude skipping work this morning could be a sign he'd gotten an early Christmas present last night.

****

David pulled the car in front of Mary's house. He wouldn't be surprised when she didn't invite him in. She never asked him in her house. Her and JT's house. Surely he had to be used to it by now. She sat in silence as she watched the for sale sign swing in the wind. She had hoped the sign would be coming down today, but she was wrong. So wrong.

"David."

"Mary, wait before you say something you'll regret. Take a couple of days to think about things." He wrapped his matching leather-gloved hand to the interior of his car around the steering wheel. "I'm a great catch. Don't lose me over some deadbeat husband who seems to care about everything but you."

Ouch. That hurt. Maybe JT wasn't the man she thought he was. Maybe she'd had the Christmas wool pulled over her eyes. Maybe she was an idiot, but that had nothing to do with David. And that was a subject she wanted to address right now. Not a couple of days from now. She'd tried several times on the ten hour drive home to talk to him about her trip, but he'd stopped her every single time.

"David." She put her hand up to halt his protest. "David, I don't need a couple of days. You see, I can't give you my heart. It doesn't belong to me anymore."

"What are you talking about?"

She released a held breath. "I love JT. Maybe he doesn't deserve it. But I do."

"Wake up. He's playing you. Trust me. I know how the game works and he was playing you for a piece of rekindling as—"

"Stop it." Mary wanted to slap him. "Don't you dare try to tell me what JT was doing. He has *nothing* to do with what I'm trying to say." Well he sort of did, but not really. "Bottom line is, I can't expect to give my heart to you or anyone else when my husband still has possession."

He snickered.

She nibbled on her bottom lip. "I'm not saying I have any expectations of a reconciliation." Big lying jerk didn't deserve one. "What I am saying is I'm not ready to move on to another relationship." *I need to fix me.*

He pulled a black box out of his pocket and flicked the lid open. The biggest diamond she'd ever seen, shined back at her. "You sure?"

Was he really bribing her with the enormous rock?

"Yes, David, I'm sure. I'm sorry."

He stared at the ring as if longing to wear it himself. "I guess I'll keep it. I'm sure I'll find someone who will be glad to accept my offer."

Really? He must have missed the chapter in the book on *Winning a Girl 101*. No one wants a ring purchased for someone else. Her turn to snicker. *Yikes.* Wonder if he'd offered the ring to someone before her? Probably. He'd said a million times he was at that point in his life where he needed to get married and start a family. He said it showed commitment in the eyes of the partners of the firm.

"David, some woman will be lucky to have you."

"I know." He sighed. "I was just hoping the woman

would be you."

Sweet. Sort of. She reached for her door handle. "Thanks for driving me home."

"No problem. I was coming this way anyway." He smiled. He pushed a button and popped the trunk. "You know the weird thing?"

Ahh, everything. "What's that?"

"Jollyville isn't on any map. Not on MapQuest. Not on GPS. I had my secretary try and make a travel plan for me, and she said the place didn't exist."

"Well, obviously it does."

"I don't know. The only reason I found it was because I lucked into it. I followed a mail truck in. It's not on the map."

Mary collapsed back in her seat. Then it all made perfect sense. She turned her gaze to him and smiled. "Well of course it isn't. How would Santa get any work done if people knew where to find him?"

"Excuse me?" David looked at her as if she had two heads.

"Nothing." She held in a laugh. "I was only joking."

Sort of.

****

Mary was pouring her mother a cup of coffee the next morning when the phone rang. Her heart palpitated as she answered, refusing to admit she hoped the call was JT.

"Hello."

"Hello, Mary. It's Jay Townsend."

Nope. Total opposite of JT. Her divorce lawyer.

"You are going to love me."

"Yeah?"

"Yes, ma'am. I ran into Judge Carter at the country club and talked him into going into the office for an hour on Christmas Eve to sign your divorce papers."

She could hear the arrogance in his voice. "Merry Christmas. You will be divorced in four days."

Yay. Just what every girl is hoping for on Christmas morning. Proof she's a failure.

She thanked her attorney anyway and hung up the phone.

"Who was on the phone?" Her mother asked as she settled in at the kitchen table.

"My lawyer. Seems I don't have to wait for my divorce to be final until the first of the year, after all." She wrapped her fingers around her coffee cup. "Mom, I know you're disappointed, but your gift didn't work."

"Hmmm. That's a shame. The woman sounded so confident."

She wondered if the woman referred to was Joy Klaus. She looked at her mother. "Mom. I never should have gone on the trip in the first place." A warm tingling feeling stirred in her belly. "I should have done what JT suggested I do for years." She frowned.

Here it goes.

"I should have stood up to you, Mom."

Her mom's expression hardened. "What on earth are you talking about?"

She sighed. "Mom, I love you so much. But since I was ten years old, I've done everything in my power to please you. I've given in to your every whim."

Her mom turned her head away. Was that guilt Mary saw flash across her face?

"I've always said yes to you. Even when I should have said no."

Her mom rolled her eyes. "So, what's so wrong with saying yes to your mother?"

"I was trying to make up for the pain Dad caused you." Mary shrugged a shoulder. "But it wasn't my place. I had nothing to do with Dad leaving."

It was the truth. It wasn't her fault.

"It wasn't my fault." Saying the words out loud freed Mary from years of guilt and bondage. Her heart raced and her eyes blurred with tears. "It wasn't my fault," she repeated.

"I know it wasn't your fault." Her mother crossed her arms over her chest. "It was that pig I was married to for twenty years' fault."

Mary straightened in her chair.

"That man was a womanizer from the day we said "I do." Her mom huffed. "It was only a matter of time before some tramp came along and stole him away." Her lips thinned. "And good riddance to him."

Mary couldn't believe this. "Mom, if daddy was always a jerk, why did you let me go for years feeling sorry for you?" Mary pushed her chair out and stood. "I blamed myself. If I hadn't had the birthday party, daddy wouldn't have gotten drunk and kissed that horrible woman."

Mary's mother waved her back to her seat. "Sit down, Mary."

Mary reluctantly slid back in her chair and folded her hands in front of her.

Her mom twisted her lips before speaking. "I know you've always let me…"

"Control me."

Her mother shot her a *watch it* glare. "…have my way." She flew her hand around in a small circle. "It was nice to feel important."

"Mom. Important. Really?" Mary sighed. "I never said no to you. You were so sad after Dad left, I swore I would never let you feel that way again. So I always said yes to you and your silly requests." She glared. "Like a week at the Rekindle Inn." She shook her head. "I was finally starting to have some semblance of a life, after the separation. I went actual weeks without crying."

She tapped her fingers on the table then glared at her mother. "But now it's like the wound in my heart has been ripped wide open, and the judge is going to scatter salt into it for me as an early Christmas present."

Her mom slipped her hands around her daughter's. "I'm sorry, honey. I should have stayed out of it." Her mom sniffed. "We were sure you two still loved each other. We assumed you were letting pride stand in your way." Her mom squeezed Mary's fingers.

Mary looked into her eyes.

"We were only trying to give you two a chance to talk it out." Tears rolled down her mother's cheeks at a steady pace. "I'm sorry, Mary. It was a stupid idea. We should have minded our own business."

It actually had been a marvelous idea. One that had worked. For a little while. She bit at her shaking lip. If only JT wasn't a liar like her father. Stupid Whitney Conner. Why did he lie about seeing her? It wasn't like she had any say so anymore. Shoot. For that matter, she was seeing David before the trip. Then it dawned on her.

Chances of Mary jumping in bed with JT knowing he'd been with her nemesis would have narrowed his chances to...zero. That's why he'd lied. Stupid jerk.

****

Mary poured herself a glass of wine and crawled onto the sofa in front of the fireplace to open Christmas cards. She was amazed at how many people thought she and JT were still together. She separated JT's friends and family from hers as best she could. She'd drop them off at his parents'. She didn't want to see him. Not now.

She arrived at one name she didn't recognize. Daniels. She opened the envelope and withdrew a card with a picture of Santa Claus on the front. An identical resemblance to Nick.

There was a long, hand-written note inside.

Dear Mr. and Mrs. Walker,

I couldn't let this holiday go by without thanking you again. If it wasn't for you, Mr. Walker, this could have been a horrible Christmas for me and my family. I'm happy to report Marcus has made huge improvements with his physical therapy.

Mary looked at the envelope again. The letter was so personal. Surely they had the wrong Walkers.

The doctors are confident he will take his first steps by New Year's Day. And Marcus is determined. He will succeed. You know how hard-headed he can be. We still find amusement in the midst of the tragedy when I recollect the events of that day to Marcus. The panic that overcame you when my water broke in the emergency room.

What in the world? This had to be a mistake. Mary was riddled in guilt for reading the intimate note from someone she'd never met, but couldn't stop herself from finishing.

I grabbed onto your hand so tight I'm surprised

you didn't have broken bones, too. We will always be thankful to you, Mr. Walker. You saved our family that day. You were our miracle. If you hadn't come by the jobsite when you did, they would have never found Marcus crushed under those beams. If you hadn't been in the emergency room with me giving me strength, when I went into labor, I'm not sure our son would have come into this world alive. He will be six months old on Christmas Eve. We named him after you. Joseph Marcus Daniels.

Mary's heart-rate escalated in her chest as she backtracked the months. Six months ago would have been the 24th of June. The day she flew out on their honeymoon trip. Alone. Why didn't he call her to explain?

Because she'd cut her phone off. She'd only left it on long enough to tell JT their marriage was over and he could go to hell—*in a voicemail*.

She put the cards aside and picked up her phone. She'd dialed the first two numbers of JT's phone number when Whitney Conner's text flashed before her. She tossed the phone on the cushion beside her. *No. Too late.* None of it even mattered anymore.

Chapter 14

Kyle sat on the couch glaring at JT.

"What?"

"What? Hell, dude, you did it again." Kyle brushed a hand through his hair. "You let Mary go without defending yourself. *Again*."

"If she loved me, there wouldn't be anything to defend." He stood and paced the room. "Plus ,she'd already called Dorky Dave and told him it was a big mistake. I…was a mistake."

"You're going to believe that jerk?"

JT stopped pacing and leaned a hand against the mantel, staring into the fire burning below. "I don't know, man. You should have seen the ring. Why would she want me when she could have Jaguar boy and his tons and tons of money?"

Kyle smirked. "Oh, I don't know. Maybe because she *loves you*. Maybe because everyone knows lawyers are a bunch of stuffed shirts."

It was clear Kyle was aggravated with JT. And JT couldn't blame him. Maybe he should have explained that Whitney's text was taken out of context. Or maybe he should have hunted Mary down the day after Marcus's accident. He knew the travel agency she usually used; he could have found her if he tried.

He swiped his hand over his eyes. God, he was exhausted. This emotional crap could really drain a guy.

"I don't know, Kyle. I don't know why I didn't." He went to the closest chair and collapsed in it. "I guess I always thought she deserved better than me anyway."

"What the hell are you talking about? You're like one of the coolest dudes I know."

He couldn't help but laugh. Kyle was a good friend. "Well. I'm not sure I'm cool enough for her."

"Dude, you should let her decide for herself." Kyle crossed an ankle over his knee. "You got to deal with your old man. He's got you all whacked out, thinking you're not good enough." He tossed a pillow sitting on the couch and hit JT in the head. "I think you have daddy issues."

He smirked. "Screw you, man." He knew Kyle was joking, but only a little. He did have daddy issues. And it was about time he dealt with them. He stood and glared at Kyle. "I think I'm going to go have a talk with my old man."

"Yes!" Kyle jumped up and bumped fist with JT. "That's what I'm talking about."

He grabbed his keys and was about to open the door when Kyle yelled over his shoulder. "And get your wife back while you're at it."

One thing at a time. One thing at a time.

He opened the door. Whitney had parked in the driveway behind his truck. Perfect. Now he didn't need to find her.

"Hey." She grinned as she walked toward him. "Daddy told me you were back."

"Yep."

He met her at the end of the sidewalk.

"You heading out?" Whitney stuck her hands in her pockets. Playing coy.

"Yep." He crossed his arms over his chest. "I was coming to find you, actually."

Her eyes grew large and her face lit up. "Great. You don't have to go far." She started walking toward him, and he put his hand up to stop her.

"I was coming to tell you to stop calling and texting me."

Her shoulders arched and her expression sobered. "What?"

There wasn't an easy way around this, so he chose brutal honesty. "Whitney. My wife read your text and saw the five missed calls. You made something innocent seem very guilty."

She crossed her arms. "Your wife? I thought that was over." She arched her dark brows. "In fact, word is she has a new hot lawyer boyfriend."

Hot? Really? More nerdy looking than anything. But he decided he probably looked at David through *get your slimy hands off my wife* husband eyes.

"Bottom line, Whit, you've got to move on. Sorry if I sound like an ass, but we will never get back together."

He waited for her head to start spinning and the threats. There were always threats.

"Screw you, JT Walker." Her jaw tightened. "I just felt sorry for you." Her eyes narrowed. "We *have* been friends for years."

He tilted his head. "No. Not really."

"How can you say that? I come to see you every time I'm in town visiting my family."

"Ah, nope. You just tell everyone in town that, to make sure it gets back to Mary."

She rolled her eyes. "So what? She deserved it. She

stole you from me."

"Again—no. We were done way before I met her."
He ran a hand through his hair. "Anyway, no reason to
hash all this up. I want you to please leave me alone.
Leave my wife alone."

"So you think you can be a jerk to me and I'm not
going to say anything to Daddy?"

He shrugged. "I don't care if you say anything to
Daddy." He'd been worried about that for years. Maybe
that's why he tolerated her all this time. Not anymore.
He walked to his truck and reached for the handle.

"You better care because in about two minutes you
will no longer have a job." She pulled her phone out of
her pocket and started dialing.

"Do you mind moving your car?" His casual
attitude seemed to up her aggravation.

"Daddy. Fire JT. Fire him now."

He gestured a finger for her to move her car out of
the way.

"Because he is being horrible to me. He's telling
me to never call him again. He's being so mean."

If only she could hear how stupid and spoiled she
sounded.

JT jumped in the driver seat, closed the door, and
rolled down the window. "Are you going to be long? I
really have someplace to be." He wasn't sure why he
egged her on. But it was kind of fun.

Clearly, Whitney wasn't getting the response from
her father she wanted. "Daddy, don't
you...Daddy...Daddy?" She pulled the phone away
from her ear and stared at it.

Yep. Clearly he'd hung up on her. She shot JT one
last evil glare before jumping in her car and speeding

away.

God, that felt good. He'd been wanting to do that since high school.

His phone rang. He looked at the name on the caller ID. Mr. Conner. "Hello."

"JT, what the hell is going on? Please tell my you're not quitting."

"No, sir. Just setting boundaries with your daughter."

The man sighed deep into the phone. "Good. Someone needs to." His tone calmed. "Well then. You have a Merry Christmas. See you at the first of the year."

"Yes, sir. Merry Christmas to you, too."

He hung up the phone. One down. Two to go.

****

JT walked into his parents' house and was greeted with Christmas chaos. Some people were decorating, others carried in food trays. His mom and dad didn't hurt for money, but they weren't super rich, either. His mom always went all out for her Christmas Eve party, starting preparations days in advance.

He walked down the long foyer and made his way to the large kitchen at the back of the house. Champagne fountains lined the counters along with boxes of other stuff. His mom was engrossed in fixing a centerpiece that looked as if it had lost a few pieces.

"Hey, Mom."

When she looked up a smile grew across her face. "Hi, Son." She hurried toward him with open arms. "When did you get back?" She held him in a bear hug as she shot off her list of twenty questions. "How was it? Was it as beautiful as the brochure described? Was

Mary happy? How is Mary? Is she here?"

He gently pulled free. "Wow. How can you ask so many questions without taking a breath?"

She stared up into her son's eyes. "Oh, it's easy. Years of practice." She shook a finger at him. "But you haven't answered a single one."

"I've got one for you, instead. Where's Dad?"

"He's in his office. You know he hides from now until it's time for the party."

She was right about that. His dad was an obedient husband and stayed out of her way until it was safe to resurface again. JT kissed his mom's cheek. "It's good to see you, Mom."

"Likewise baby-cakes." She returned to her pitiful centerpiece.

He found his dad in his office, just where she'd said he'd be. He rested in a high-backed leather chair with his legs crossed and his head tilted back. Eyes closed. *Hmmm. Sleeping in the middle of the day. Strange.* JT didn't disturb him. Instead, he leaned against the doorjamb and took a closer look. His father had aged. He was still pretty fit for sixty-four, but the years definitely showed in the crow's feet around his eyes and the gray streaking his hair. When did his dad get…old?

His dad startled awake. He looked surprised to see JT. "Joseph. I didn't expect to see you there."

"I didn't mean to wake you, Dad."

His father waved him in. "No. No. Just resting my eyes, that's all. Have you seen your mother? Lord, she's been busting at the seams, waiting for you to get back. Hoping and praying the inn was as good as they claimed it to be."

JT settled in a chair. "They're pretty special, that's for sure."

His father's face beamed. "So it worked? Well I'll be darned." His father fiddled with the crease in his pants. "I considered it to be a bunch of poppycock myself. Guess I was wrong."

"Well, I wouldn't say it worked, exactly."

His father's eyes narrowed and his grin faded.

There it was. The look of disappointment JT recognized so well. "Dad. I need to talk to you man-to-man."

His dad perked up. "Is that right?"

JT nodded.

"Well, in that case, I guess I better pour us a drink." His father went to the decanter of liquor on the side table, and poured two glasses of whisky. He handed one to his son, then tapped his glass against JT's. "Toast to talking man-to-man."

Was it trepidation or dread he saw flash across his father's face? JT waited for his father to settle back in his chair.

"Dad. Do you think I'll ever do anything to make you proud of me?"

His father's face scrunched up as if he'd just tasted something bitter. "JT, what on earth are you talking about?"

He propped his elbows on his knees. He swirled the brown liquid around in his glass. "Just what I said. I'm thirty-one years old, and I can't think of one time when something I did was good enough." He brought the glass to his lips and took a big swallow. The burn ran from his throat and landed somewhere in the emptiness of his stomach. Getting that question out in the open felt good. Finally asking what he'd been wondering his entire life. He waited for the explosion. But it didn't come.

"Son, I guess I owe you an apology."

His gaze shot to his father. Where was the anger? He didn't look mad at all. In fact, he almost looked sad.

"Joseph, I've been proud of you every day of your life."

What? JT smirked. He had to be joking. "Dad, how can you say that? Every game, every report card, it was…'Joseph, this is good, but you can do better.'"

"I wanted you to strive to be the best you could be."

"The best I could be for me or for you?" He placed his glass on the table and stood. He paced. "I always seemed to let you down." JT brushed a hand through his hair. "Hell, I'm one of the best contractors in the area. I *am* the best that I can be, and I still feel like you're disappointed."

"Why?"

"Because you always pushed medical school. You were so mad when I told you I didn't want to be a doctor like you."

"I wasn't mad. I was a little disap—"

"Disappointed." Their gazes locked. "Bingo."

His father took a moment before he spoke. Almost as if he were choosing his words very carefully. "No, Joseph. Not disappointed in you. Disappointed for the medical field itself. You are so good at whatever you set your mind to, I knew you'd make an exceptional physician."

His father took his glass and emptied it in one swallow. "I wasn't disappointed in you, son. How could

I be? You excelled in everything you did. You never got into trouble." His father's mouth curved. "Other than the time you and Kyle broke the neighbor's fence, sneaking into their pool."

JT remembered the night well. He was sure his dad would kill them. But he didn't. He had the fence repaired and never ratted them out to his mom. In fact, come to think of it, that was the same year his dad had their own pool put in.

His father hurried to the side table and poured another drink. "You've never given me or your mother anything but joy."

He knew he hadn't imagined it. His dad was tough on him. Always.

"I'm afraid I have to disappoint you now, though." JT sighed.

His dad stared back at him.

"I didn't get Mary back. I tried, Dad. I really did." He leaned against the desk. "For a little while, it was actually perfect." He smiled at the memory of holding her in his arms. "But I lost her again."

His father walked over to JT and placed a firm hand on his shoulder. "Son. I've made a mess of things. I should have told you how important you were to me and how much I loved you. Instead, I had you believing I didn't love you enough." A frown crossed his father's face. "I'm sorry."

The tears of regret JT saw fill his father's eyes were like a wakeup call. He'd made the same mistake with Mary. He told her a thousand times he loved her, but he never showed her how much he loved her. He didn't tell her how important she was to him. He didn't tell her when she kicked him out that his life was over.

He didn't tell her he was nothing without her.

He reached in and grabbed his father. "I love you, Dad."

His father embraced him with a strong hug. "I love you, too, son. You make me proud *every day*."

His father's words echoed in his mind. Words he'd waited his entire life to hear. Contentment filled him. "Thanks, Dad. That means a lot." Everything became crystal clear.

He pulled away from his father. "Dad, I've got to go."

"Where are you going?"

"I've got to go win my wife back."

His father's face lit up and he patted JT on the shoulder. "Well, go. Go get her, son."

"That's my plan." He rushed out the door. It would actually be helpful if he had *a plan.*

****

JT sighed. He felt strange knocking on his own front door. Luckily he didn't have to stand there long. Only a second or two elapsed before the porch light glared in his face. Maybe he should have called first. Mary looked through the side glass, then opened the door.

"JT, what are you doing here?"

He opened his mouth to speak but empty air followed. The million things he'd practiced on the way over escaped him.

"Well?"

"Can we talk?"

She hesitated, then backed away from the door so he could pass. He stepped inside and followed her to the kitchen. She grabbed a bottle of wine and emptied the remaining contents into her glass.

"I'd offer you a glass, but it appears I'm out." She said shaking the last few drops over her wineglass. "I'm celebrating." There was a hint of a slur when she spoke.

"Yeah? What are you celebrating?"

She swerved a tiny bit when she walked and turned to face him. "To new beginnings." She hoisted her glass, almost hitting his chin. "In fourteen hours, I will be divorced." Her eyes narrowed. "You should have a glass. You'll be divorced, too."

JT took the glass from her and placed it on the table. He grabbed her hand and pulled her gently to the sofa. "We need to talk."

She plopped on the sofa without much resistance. "*Now* you have something to say?"

He swallowed his nerves. *Just spill your guts.*

"Mary. I should have told you in Jollyville, the text you read from Whitney was her exaggerating a pool game we played the night before I left for the inn. That was the *first* time I had run into her outside of work since she'd moved back." He looked into her eyes. "I don't want Whitney Conner." He turned his gaze to the floor. "I didn't think you'd believe me, so I left."

"Why didn't you tell me about Marcus Daniels?"

His gaze flew to hers. "How do you know about that?"

She reached for a Christmas card on the table and held it out to him. "They named their baby after you."

Really? No way.

"Why didn't you tell me about the accident?"

He stuck his hands in his pockets and shrugged. "Stupidity. Pride. I don't know?" He released a long breath. "At that point, we were pretty shot anyway. You were so damn mad in your voicemail." He tilted his chin a notch. "You wouldn't have listened."

She pulled her legs up and wrapped her arms around them. "You're right." She frowned. "I wouldn't have listened."

"Mary, I've made some stupid mistakes. I should have told you how much I loved you. I only worked so hard to prove myself worthy of you."

She shook her head. "Stop." She raised a palm. "Please stop, JT. You weren't the only one who's to blame." She glanced at him then looked away. "I kept one bag packed, ready for you to cheat on me. I just knew all men were like my father." Silence danced in the air as tears trickled down her cheeks. Her eyes found his once more. "You didn't stand a chance."

What was she saying? Could they start over? "Let me make it up to you."

She wiped her eyes on her sleeve. "No. It's too late."

He walked over and knelt before her. "No. It's not. We screwed up. But we're not those same two insecure people." He brushed at a strand of blonde hair that had fallen over her face and tucked it gently behind her ear. "The inn changed us."

She placed a soft hand over his, but she shook her head. His chest caved in. This couldn't be the end. She had to understand.

"It's over for us, JT." Her eyes were blurred with tears, but he knew she meant it.

He couldn't hold his head up. He was paralyzed with grief. This wasn't happening.

"JT, I'm going to the judge's office tomorrow, and I'm signing the divorce papers."

She kissed the top of his head. "I will always love you. And I'm so sorry for the part I played in the hurt we've suffered. But we can't go back." She stood and he grasped her leg, not wanting to let her go. He knew if she walked away she'd be walking away for good.

She pulled her leg free. "I will always cherish the Rekindle Inn." Her words were barely audible through her tears. "Please lock the door behind you." She ran from the room and up the stairs. To disappear from his sight. His life.

This wasn't real. He'd played this scene out a million times in his mind on the way over, and it always ended with them back together. Never with him leaving and…locking the door behind him.

Chapter 15

Mary woke to her alarm buzzing. *Please shut up.* She slapped a hand on the button to deafen the annoying sound. She winced. Her head rang a tad, too. Then the empty wine bottle came to mind. That explained the pounding in her brain. She'd always been a two-glass girl. She lifted her head from the pillow.

Ouch. Now she remembered why.

Then a flashback of JT kneeling in front of her surfaced. She tried to retrieve the conversation but it came in foggy clumps.

Shower. Now.

She forced herself to crawl out of bed and into the bathroom. She was glad she did. The shower worked wonders on her achy head and her muddled memory. Now it was her heart that ached. In four hours, her marriage would be nothing but a memory filed in the clerk's office. She slipped on her robe and crawled back under the covers. Yay for having a lawyer who shared the same country club as her judge. Her lips turned downward and she tried hard not to cry. "Merry Christmas to me."

Thud.

Mary jumped at the odd noise.

Thud.

There it was again. The sound originated from outside. She slowly walked to the window. She raised the blinds and looked out.

JT. He leaned against his truck, his hand holding something large and white. Her pulse beat faster. What was he doing in front of her house? He held up a sign and Mary fell to her knees; her wobbly legs unable to hold her weight.

I love you, Mary.

When he swapped the sign for another, her heart stopped beating.

Let me be your hero.

Her heart literally burned with love when he swapped out the signs again.

Will you stay married to me?

Her head fell to her hands. She couldn't stop the sobs. He still loved her. He still loved her. God, she loved him, too. She could pretend all she wanted that she didn't, but the truth was she still loved him to heaven and back.

Tears ran uncontrollably down her cheeks. Her head bobbed back to the window. He stared up at her. Waiting for her answer.

Yes. Yes.

"Yes, I will stay married to you." She screamed through the glass. Her fingers rushed to unlock the latch on the window but it wouldn't budge. She pounded on the window. "Don't leave. I'm coming."

She jumped to her feet and ran to her dresser. She yanked open the drawer and grabbed a pair of sweats and slipped them on. She reached for a t-shirt from another drawer and pulled the top over her head as she hurried down the steps.

Mary was halfway down the stairs when she stopped. She turned and rushed back to her room. She jerked open her jewelry box. Her wedding rings sat inside. Lying in the same corner where she'd left them months ago. She pushed them on her shaking finger and ran down the stairs.

Mary slung open the door. She hopped down the steps, and sprinted across the yard barefoot. Her feet were immediately frozen, but she didn't care. She didn't slow when she reached JT. Instead, she leaped in the air and jumped in his arms. Her legs wrapped around his waist. He pulled her body into his, sliding his hands under her bottom.

"Yes," she said between kisses. "Yes. I will stay married to you."

He twirled her before coming to a stop. His big blue gaze settled on hers. He leaned down and their lips merged. His kiss was warm. Passionate. Mind-boggling. He broke the kiss and stared down at her.

"I'll never make you sorry, babe. I promise you. You will never doubt how much I love you, because I'll prove it to you, every day for the rest of my life."

She laughed. "Sounds perfect. I love you so much, JT." The warmth of tears settled in the back of her eyes.

Chapter 16

They reached his parents' party late and for good reason. They'd spent the day taking down the for sale sign, calling lawyers and, well…rekindling things. But they'd arrived, ready to shock the parents with their reconciliation.

He helped her with her coat and handed it to the person taking them at the door. "They're going to flip." Mary looked up at him. Excitement danced across her cheeks.

"Look at that. Your blush matches the red dress you're wearing." He squeezed her hand. "Mary, I know I've told you already, but you look absolutely beautiful."

He had told her a hundred times, and every time she loved hearing it. "Thanks." She glanced down at herself. "I picked up this dress from a very unusual dress shop in Jollyville."

"I'm glad you did. It looks like it was made for you."

Her gaze locked with his.

Mrs. Walker, the day you put on this dress your life will be full of happiness.

"What is it?"

She tilted her head. "I was just recalling what the saleswoman said to me the day I bought it." She blinked away the memory. "Just more crazy Christmas town magic I guess."

A squeal came from the end of the foyer and they turned to the commotion. "It worked. It worked." JT's mom embraced Mary's mother.

His father tossed his hands in the air. "Good Lord. Now they'll take the credit for years to come." He hurried to them, wrapping them in his arms.

"It's okay, Dad." JT smiled at his wife. "They do deserve some credit."

"Welcome home." Mr. Walker placed a gentle kiss on Mary's cheek.

She was home. Back with her husband. Her family. Her life.

The rest of the night became a glorious interval of dancing, eating, drinking champagne. She was happy. So happy. Mary grinned. For the first time since her father left, she truly trusted happiness.

JT rounded the corner and grabbed her hand. "You've got to see this." He dragged her down the long hallway and didn't stop until they reached his parents' huge living room.

Good grief. Where was the fire? He led her to the family Christmas tree.

"What is it?"

He pointed to the tree. "Look."

She followed the direction that his finger pointed. She saw the ornaments and gasped. Their ornaments. The signs and the little arm cast hung side by side. "How did they get here?"

"I don't know. I asked Mom if she hung them there, and she said she'd never seen them before."

Wow. She nibbled on her bottom lip. *Wow.*

Mary sensed the familiar tingling all over, like

when she was in Jollyville.

"Do you feel it?" His gaze settled over hers.

She nodded. "Yep." She felt it all right. Something shiny caught Mary's attention. A beautifully wrapped present waited on the table beside the tree. She wasn't sure how she knew, but the gift was left for them. "Look."

He picked up the gift and opened the small card attached. "Mary and Joseph. Merry Christmas, you two. Nick." He arched a brow. "How in the world did he get—"

"Open it." She couldn't stand the suspense.

He ripped off the paper and handed the box to her. Their eyes met for a moment before she lifted the lid. Inside was a crystal ornament of a family standing in front of the Rekindle Inn. A father, a mother, and a baby.

"Kind of strange considering it was only the two—" Her attention redirected itself to her belly. Her gaze flew to his. She stopped taking the pill when they broke up. She hadn't needed birth control.

Oh. My. Goodness.

"What is it, Mary? What's going on?"

Her face lit. "I'm not sure how I know this, but I'm pretty sure I'm…"

"You're what?" His face filled with concern. "What, Mary? You're what?"

She nibbled on her bottom lip for courage. "Pregnant," she whispered. Her forehead wrinkled as she waited his response. Not sure what it would be.

One eye lifted to sneak a peek at his reaction. He looked…shocked. Speechless. Stunned. His blank deer-in-the-headlight look was almost cute but left her feeling nervous.

"Say something." She wrung her fingers together. "I could be wrong. It's only a feeling." *Good grief, say something.* Worry hit her over the head. How could she be pregnant now? They still needed to sort out their relationship. She rubbed her tight neck.

She didn't see the grin slide across his lips. "Mary, this is great news."

Her gaze flew to his. "It is?"

"Yes. In fact it's the best Christmas present I could've ever asked for."

Her lips curved. Tears filled her lashes as she bobbed her head in agreement. "A baby. Yep. Best present ever."

His arms enfolded her in a tight hug. "Merry Christmas, Mary. I love you."

Her heart exploded with contentment. "I love you, too, JT." She leaned in and placed a soft kiss on his lips. "Merry Christmas."

A word about the author...

Lori Waters writes amusing, heartfelt contemporary romance. She is the 2014 TARA Award Winner in the Series Contemporary category for *Christmas at the Rekindle Inn.*

Though she grew up on the shores of Virginia, she now lives with her family, including her little dog Max, in a small town in North Carolina. She is a member of Romance Writers of America and Carolina Romance Writers.

Follow her at www.loriwatersauthor.com and www.badgirlzwrite.com and on Twitter @loriwaters6 http://www.loriwatersauthor.com